T·H·E WORRY WORRY WORRY GIRL

Other books by the author:

This Place

THE WORRY WORRY WORRY GIRL

STORIES FROM A CHILDHOOD

ANDREA FREUD LOEWENSTEIN

Firebrand
Books
Ithaca, New York

Book design by Betsy Bayley
Cover design by Lisa Cowden and Betsy Bayley
Typesetting by Bets Ltd.

Printed in the United States on acid-free paper by McNaughton & Gunn

Author's Disclaimer:
Although I have retained the Freud name in this book as an essential back-
drop, it is a work of fiction. None of the characters are actual people, living
or dead, and the events portrayed, like the characters, are fictional composites
of memory, imagination, and invention.

Library of Congress Cataloging-in-Publication Data

Loewenstein, Andrea Freud.
　　The worry girl : stories from a childhood / by Andrea Freud
Loewenstein.
　　　　p.　　cm.
　　ISBN 1–56341–017–6 (cloth). — ISBN 1–56341–016–8 (pbk.)
　　I. Title.
　　PS3562.O4W6　　1992
　　813'.54—dc20
　　　　　　　　　　　　　　　　　　　　　　　　　　　92–8021
　　　　　　　　　　　　　　　　　　　　　　　　　　　CIP

ACKNOWLEDGMENTS

I AM GRATEFUL TO THE FOLLOWING WOMEN:

Joy Holland, whose unfailing love and acceptance gave me the safety I needed to go back in time, and who was the first appreciative audience and insightful critic for each of these stories.

Sophie Freud, who has always wanted the very best for me and tried her hardest to see that I got it. As a fellow author she understands that my work is fiction and encourages me to publish my stories even when she remembers them quite differently.

Jan Clausen, whose story "A Privileged Childhood" enabled me to write about my own privileged childhood, and who has offered me steadfast and loving friendship and support during the writing of this book. Kate Rounds, who consistently and generously offered me concrete help and moral support. Nicky Morris, Randall Kindleberger, Adair Lynn, Amy Kass, and Ann Rhodes, each of whom has in different ways helped me to write this book.

My editor, Nancy K. Bereano, whose enthusiasm, dedication, and dependability made this book a reality.

During the writing of this book I taught at Goddard College, and students, faculty, and administration listened to early drafts and provided a supportive environment in which to write.

For my mother, Sophie Freud

CONTENTS

THE STORIES THAT CAME BEFORE

The Grandmothers' Stories

KOOKMAL, LOOK IN THE PHOTO, THE SEATS, THE LAKE, ZO *GEMUTLICH*. LOOK HOW WE MAKE HERE A nice picnic, a little herring, a little cucumber zalade—come, Puppi you're hungry? Oma will bring you something, some t-wurst, some whitefish. See, in the photo comes here Anna bringing us to eat a little something. A nice girl, Anna, from the village, a simple girl. Always came the villagers, if they needed something, if they had a problem, always they said, "Frau K. knows how to act with a servant, she knows how to make nice." Look, such a white stone house we had, so big, and from all around came the people to meet with your Opa, they loeved him s-o-o much. You remember, Papa? Even from other countries they came, from France, from America, and sometimes I cooked for them, we had always a cook, but just to make a little special you understand, because your Opa wanted. When he wanted something, I wanted it also, never mind how hard I

9

had to work, nicht so, Papa? Not like your mother. And in the end it was one of your Opa's colleagues from America who had been many times to eat in our house who made the papers, so we could come here. Before the war, about Jews we never spoke so much, why should we, after all, we were not religious, aber zo, we didn't eat pig, how do you say snail? Creb? But that was just costume, nein? In the rest we were German, why not, your Opa was a German officer when I met him. In his uniform, with his blue eyes, so tall, so hendsome! I come also you know from a prominent family, maybe not so famous like your mother's family but a good family, very well off. For some reason, I don't know why, the young men always came to our house to see me, the other girls were so eifersuochtig, so jealous! They said I was ein a schoenes Mädchen, a pretty girl, you know. But the first time I saw your Opa was enough, from that moment I knew already, this one I will marry. He felt also the same way. From that day we loe—v, from that day we always agree, yah, Papi? And this I have never regretted. For you, we want the same, one day. Come, let Oma fix a little your hair, so struwwel kopf you look!

◈

    From the beginning I had the ambition to go on the stage, in Vienna you understand, on the stage in Vienna, this is something special, not like the dreck they have here, zo *scheuszlich,* someone tried to give to me last week, this Mrs. Knockwurst, you remember, with the double chin, a ticket to Broadway, some old ticket for a play she didn't any more want. I don't go to such garbage I told her, I have with my time better things to do. Look, here is how I was then, in evening dress, when I made my first recitation, I was a most beautiful woman, you can see that, yah? Your old grandmother which nobody wants around was once a most beautiful, elegant woman, very much admired, from the very best family. You cannot imagine the flowers I had in the dressing room that night, from the finest florist in Vienna, roses, orchids from my admirers. I had a talent, this everyone but my mother was forced to agree, even one of the most famous men in Vienna, Herr Z., when he saw me perform, he became one of my admirers. You cannot imagine such a thing, you with your mother who would do anything for you, but my mother was a dissatisfied woman, her own life had been ruined, completely a rack and ruin I tell you, and she tried to make of my life the same, but you see how it is, she did not succeed—in the end, I became der Doctor Freud in spite of all of them.

Listen, this is how it was with her. She had a grandiose singing voice, a soprano, also she was beautiful—such gifts which do not often meet in one person—and so she made a concert, not to get money you understand, just for show, and it was a *merveil,* a *succès sensationnel.* After this to her came one day a telegram from the Berlin staatsopera, offering to her a contract, and her Papa—he intercepted it! It was not the way for a well brought-up girl of good family, a wealthy girl in the Jewish ghetto, you understand, it was not what was done. Soon after she married, what else could she do? She always hated me, she was like a stepmother to me, not a real mother. Later she by the Nazis was caught and killed. When I wanted to go to the Gymnasium, the Vienna Gymnasium you understand, this is one of the very best schools, world renowned, and she made such a scene, ach—such a hysterical scene. She slapped and slapped me, she made the entire household to tremble. A prediction she made that I would become hunchback and blind, a curse she made on me, you understand. To my sister she was loving, but me she hated. My father was different, I was his favorite child, but she held him under her thumb with her hysteria, what could he do? For me she wanted only to arrange a match that would make her look good. I tried always so hard to please her, you understand, I was a good daughter—even a Freud I found to marry—but for her even this was not good enough. Of the other young Jewish men I knew then, half were killed in the first war. To reward their efforts, the Nazis later put the survivors and the families of the dead into concentration camps and murdered them, you understand? Gazzed them in the ovens. This is how life is, this soon you will find out for yourself.

Your Opa with his blue eyes, no one could tell, he was just German to them. Your Daddy too has the same blue eyes, and as a boy, so blond, you remember, Papa? I wanted at least one of you should get such a blond hair, but you are all so like— ach never mind. As a child he was like an angel, your daddy, everyone when they see him they said it, and such a good boy, but too schwäche Nerven, how do you say it, too tender in the nerfs, in the heart. And such a good Papa he is to you, just like your Opa, but not so strict. Your Opa, with his children always he was just, but when he decided something, so it was. Once, only when Berthe was small, maybe five, six years, she wouldn't eat, about everything on the table, she had to make a discussion. So one day we have fresh from the lake a nice big fish, ein Karpfen, and right away she said, "No no, Mama, this fish ich kann das nicht essen, I can't eat him, look how he looks at me with his yellow eyes!" Then your Opa got angry, he took her in the room to how do you say—spenk—not hard you know, just a little spenk, but your Daddy beat with his little hands on the door, *cnack, cnack, cnack!* "Nein, nein Papa, beat me, beat me instead." So much your Daddy loeved his little sister, so-o-o much. It was like that in our family, nicht, Papa, always we loev, never we had a bad word. Your mutter, she comes from a different family. What could I say, he was a big man, it was not any more my business.

❖

When the next war came, from such a family, you think even once they helped me? From Herr Professor one could not expect, he was after all a great genius, he had to worry about many other things, and also he was already very ill at this time, but die Anna? Or die Burlingham? No, they turned their backs on me. I was too pretty for the family, this is what I heard Herr Professor say out from the corner of his mouth when my husband first brought me home. My hearing has always been acute, they try to hide things from me but I know. You see how it is with me now, how when I came to visit they reserve for me an old bed with corn cobs inside, I, a Freud! But ach, such a Freud

I got when I married, a ladies' man, and ein Geizhals! A miser! I brought with me an inheritance from my father, from the beginning I paid always for myself. The Family was always afraid I would cost them, but I earned from the beginning every penny, and my husband gambled it away. Then, when I had my children came the Family and said I could not care for them properly, and they sent a Fräulein they selected. Nothing I did was right in their eyes, you understand? They could have helped me, nein? Later, in New York, you think it was so easy for me, in my third language, to start from the beginning again ? You think someone helped me to become a Doctor? Die Anna from the beginning, from a girl she was encouraged to study, but I had to do it on my own, always on my own. Did you know that once came the Nazis to take your grandfather, but I talked to them, they were men, I smiled, I slipped to them a thousand francs, I saved his life you understand, not only once but several times, and what thanks he gave me? He left me without a penny. Then came fifteen years ago the first letter, the first one, can you imagine? After all those years he wrote to ask me for a divorce, he wants now all of a sudden to marry one of his whores. He will never have his divorce from me, never until death!

◈

There came a time, not such a nice time, that we will not talk so much about, your father as a young man, a teenager, came into the hands of the Nazis. This was in a camp in France, we didn't know where he was, if we would ever to see him again. So they came, and my brother, your Opa's brother, the children, everyone—like that, they came, and after—about this we don't need to speak so much. You can imagine, always I was thinking about mein Kind, I didn't sleep, I didn't eat, only mein Kind, my child, I wanted to find! So, one day there we stand in France, already on a train ready to go, then pulls suddenly another train into the station and suddenly, Gott sei dank, Berthe calls out, "Mama, Mama there is Brother! So quickly we jump off our train and he also jumps off, just in time. Aber until I hold him in my arms I cannot believe it is really him. And in this way—soon we can go altogether from France to New York. So lucky we were, not like so many. It's enough now. With us, all was O.K.

◈

My sister also could have helped me. She came first to New York, her husband always made for her good money, he was a nobody, a nebbish, you understand, one of these Jews who knows only money, not a man for our family, still he had plenty, he could have helped me. To find a decent man, it's not so easy, you'll see, most of them are Schweine, but your mother managed to find a good one, and you, child, must remember you are a Freud. When you meet a Jewish boy from a good family, right away you must tell him, 'Oh, by the way, I am a Freud, I am great-granddaughter of the Freuds,' like this he knows from what family you come. Listen to me, from such a family you can have anyone. Me, no one never helped, but I was at least a beautiful woman, the way you will never be with such a posture, mein Kind, the way you hold your mouth, even being a Freud will not help you, you will be hunchbacked when you grow up, if you squint like that you will be blind, no man will want you. In Paris, your mother studied in the lycée, she was a good girl from the beginning, a good daughter, and I got work, I made connections, wherever I went I managed, you see? My son was difficult, he went with der Vater, for years I didn't see him, but she I kept close to me always. You see how it is now, neither one even invited me to their wedding. Still, both my children have done well, I have no complaint. My sister's son, whom she always boasted so much—"Such a good boy, so sensitive, so loving, not like your children"—he became a schizophrenic you know. You have heard about him, yah? Your uncle, a schizophrenic. Ha!

◈

Everywhere they wanted your Opa so much, in France, in eine Fabric, a factory there, but for most it was not this way. Yah, zo, we made for them a little something, why not, nicht, Papa?

A children's dancing school we made for the dancer. A children's climbing club we made for the mountain climber. There it was he met your mother, in such a club to walk in the mountain. She was already the same, so smart, so strong in her mind, she knew exactly what she wanted, already as a little child. Never in my marriage never once I have done what *I* wanted. Always for Papa, for die Kinder, the family. Such a handsome boy, your Daddy, so many girls were always running behind him, Jewish girls and also the *schicksas,* the French, all of them wanted him, he could have had a girl what could have take care of him a little.

◈

What you need in this world is connections, yah, this you must understand. For a woman also it helps also to have a little beauty, some charm, then you can get what you need. Where comes such a posture? Has no one told you to stand straight? In that way you will get a crooked back before twenty. Open when you speak your mouth. And money, keep always some aside, always to be ready, one does not know what may happen, like that you can slip them a little something, you can get away. Look here, under the bed, in case I get again worse and have to go back in the hospital, you see such a nice cheap perfume for the nurses, this way last time I got decent care, without nothing they would leave me in pain, believe me, I could cry for water and no one would come, I know how they are, how they look at me when they think I am asleep, they treat you like dirt when you get old in this country, they all treat you like dirt. Come, pass to me my work there in the briefcase, my translation. Dr. X told me, Doctor Freud, you are not now well enough to work any more, but you see, still I work. I have always worked for what I got. No one can say I was a burden on them, you understand.

The Parents' Stories

WE WENT ALWAYS ON SUNDAY AFTERNOON

TO THE BERGASSE TO VISIT DER GROSSVATER. IT WAS A solemn occasion, an audience with a king, you see, and I was a princess. I remember very clearly the room, the old man with his beard, I was a small child, but I knew already it was important, and in this way it took on for me a double meaning, it was becoming history at the same time I was living it, this is a little interesting, no? Such a double consciousness, it's maybe something you felt too on certain occasions? It might make an interesting research maybe, to ask women what they remember of this kind, what they experienced as important events. Anyway, there I came, each Sunday, all dressed up, and he held me on his knee, only a small encounter, punctuated by the exchange of money, and this I now resent in retrospect—that my Fraulein got money and I got money, that it was such a transaction—but at the time I didn't think in this way, I wasn't as a child into questioning my life, that came only later. Once he said to me, "Have you been the best little girl in Vienna?", and after that my ambition was to be the best little girl in Vienna. I worked hard at that, it was my goal, you know how one needs a goal in life, an organizing principle.

❖

When I was a boy? Ach, never mind, I don't remember. My memory is too lousy, I must be becoming already prematurely senile. I was often worried, already at that age I had trouble sleeping. Papa was very strict, not the way he is with you children, he was a real German, with him I had always the feeling nothing I could do was good enough. Ach, never mind, it's so long ago, I can't remember, it's enough now.

Our Fraulein took care of us mostly, when we were small, but there was never a question who was in charge of our lives. I was my mother's good daughter. She sent my brother away to camp but me she took with her, everywhere—to the sea in the summer, to her resorts, where she dressed me in little outfits, in little Chinese pajamas, like a doll. I hated that, even at a young age, to be dressed up in this way, for a show piece. She and my father were always fighting, always screaming at each other, I remember once he pulled her hair and went out, to see one of his other women I think now, but then I didn't know that, and after he left she lay on the floor and kicked and screamed. I would *die* before I acted in such a way, ach, can you imagine, a grown woman to lose control, to lose one's dignity like that! It was mostly about money—he gambled, and she would scream and scream to him about money. And I think about his women also, although that was never mentioned out loud. He gave her a weekly allowance, I think now he must have been very mean. She was always short of money, and I was her confidante, her significant other, you understand? I couldn't stand it, all the time their fighting, and how she needed to pour into my ears her endless misery. And so, after a while I distanced myself from her and then she said to me, "You have a heart of stone, you are one of them—a Freud with a heart of stone." She was right, you know, I hardened my heart against her.

❖

Sorry to leave Germany? Nah, what do you mean, what are you talking about, of course not, why should I be sorry to go from a place like that? Every day on the way to school, *Jude, Jude.* Also, they threw stones. These same boys who used before to play with me. Every day in the street. But this Papa would not believe. "Garbage, nonsense, no, no, impossible they would not do this, don't lie." He believed in the Germans, he fought in the army you know, in the First War, he was a hero, but I wanted to be a French boy. You know this was where I met her first, it was in the dancing school in Paris, something they made for the Jewish refugees. Come, I teach you the song they used to sing: *Over there I was a grosse Bernardine. Over there. Over there! And here I am only a small dachsund. Over here!* I asked her with me to dance. "No." And again I met her at a mountain club, already I liked to climb, to ski. So, we climbed together up quite a high mountain, she was so small then, with such a heavy rucksack, and I asked her if I could carry it for her. "No thank you, I will carry it myself." And from that moment I knew already I would marry her.

◆

In Paris he says I met him first? Yes, probably, as children, it's quite possible. You know, in Paris what I really remember is my bicycle, it must have been my transitional object, it's funny, isn't it, how objects can become so important to one? Different objects at different life stages, more than people sometimes, they don't let you down in the same way. My mother had forbidden me to ride it, someone had told her it would be dangerous for me in the streets. So she gave me money for my lunch, and with this I paid a man in a garage to keep it for me. Every morning I picked up my bicycle and rode it to the lycée, I rode it everywhere. In this way, Paris became my city, I fell a little in love with Paris, I was happy then.

◆

I was in the hayloft in that village when she came to me, some peasant girl, I don't remember her name, I was just a boy, she was an older woman, *mmm*—such breasts, so soft, that's what a man likes in a woman, such nice big breasts. She initiated me. Ah, that was sweet. That was nice there, in the hay. That, I like to remember.

◆

It was on that same bicycle I ran from the Nazis. Mutter on her bicycle, I on mine. They were just behind us, shooting. She didn't know how to ride, she had to learn just like that, then she had to persuade someone to let us in every night, the French didn't want to, but she managed it. She was always flirting with

men, and all her costumes and her hair, and her make-up, that
charm of hers, it made me so furious then, I resented it, I vowed
never would I become a woman like that. Now, in retrospect,
I can see how she saved us, but then I wanted only to get away
from her. And my father, whom I heard not a word from, him
I missed terribly. I fantasized that he would come and get me.
She who saved me, I could not be a good daughter to, he who
left me I longed for, and that's how it is in this life, no? Unfair.
Even now, you can see how it is when she calls. My heart sinks,
sometimes I even get sick. And yet she always wanted the best
for me. She saved me, and afterwards she released me, and she
always wished me well in her heart.

◆

In France already I was a very good skier, and they had a
contest, to find out the best one. I wanted so badly at that time
to be in the ski patrol, to fight the Nazis, and they said the win-
ner of the contest would come automatically into the ski patrol. I won the contest. And then, when I went to register for
the ski patrol as they had promised, they said, come here, come
in this room to sign the papers, and this is when they grabbed
me, and took me to the camp. They were rounding up the Jews,
it was Pétain's government then—that was our first car, you
know, *Gaga Pétain.*

Ach, it wasn't so bad, nothing like the German camps, I was
young, I was very strong, but I had one good friend, he was sick,
I left him when I ran away to the village, he was in the end killed
in Auchwitz, who knows, maybe I could have taken him along.
In the village, you know already the story, how I was a big hero,
hah, a big hero for the resistance. You've been there, on the
mountain, you've seen the markers, the crosses, that was boys
from the village, they got killed, by following what I told them.
And I used to think, sometimes still I think when I can't sleep,
if only I had left them alone, they would still be alive, those boys.

◆

I was in college and I had no money at all, only what this

rich relative had given me, and you know how much I hate to take from people, to receive their condescension, but at the time I had no choice. Of course I paid it back, every penny. I had to work as a maid, a babysitter, you know the kind of people, for their lousy fifty cents they expect you to clean the whole house, I was some poor refugee to them, I should be glad to do it. It was New Year's Eve. And to eat I had only a jar of peanut butter. My English wasn't so good yet, so everything was twice as hard for me. I only got *B*'s in courses, and for me, not to get *A*'s—you can imagine! Nobody there was interested in me anyway, it was different at that time, they weren't interested in the war, in what had happened, no one wanted to talk about such things. Anyway, what did I care, I wanted nothing to do with them. I worked in Bailey's, and you know how they used to serve milkshakes—they made twice as much and gave the customer one glass and threw away the rest, such a waste! It made me sick to see how they threw away such a good milkshake, and so I drank every one. So many glasses of milkshake. I'm surprised I didn't grow fat, but of course I would not have allowed that.

◈

In America still I wanted to fight the Nazis, so I joined the Navy. Then they decided no, you can't fight, you are German, maybe who knows, you are really a Nazi spy. So, this is why in the end I sold tickets to the war. You remember, that's what I told you when you were little and you believed. By then I had found her and right away I asked her to marry me. At first she wouldn't so I asked her again and again. I would not give up, only on this one thing you understand, I would not give up.

◈

He was in the Navy, and he looked handsome in his uniform with his blue eyes, so slim a figure, not like now. And I was very lonely at this time in my life. I went on some dates with American boys, perfectly nice American Jewish boys you understand, today it would be different, but at that time they were to me like foreign creatures, another species, like if you had to go on a date with a zebra, you know what I mean? The language, always I missed the language so much. He was the same kind of animal as me, at least. He was familiar. He kept on asking me, and I would say no, no, because I thought I didn't love him enough, not really. But in the end he wore me down and I said yes. I knew he would be a good enough husband, a good enough father, that he would not leave as my father had done. And also I believed he knew so much, that he could do anything, fix anything. I was a child still, at that age, just a child.

❖

We lived in a basement first, in Washington. Cockroaches dropped from the ceiling into the soup, into our bed, plop! In the summer, we drove all across the country, in *Gaga Pétain*. Once, she was feeding the bears in Yellowstone National Park, I thought she got in, I drove on. I said to her, "Darling, what are you doing, making such a noise unwrapping the food there in the back seat?" So, I turned around, I looked in the back seat, and there was not her but a bear! We were happy before you were born, we were very happy then.

❖

I got pregnant, not because I thought it over so much, it was just what one did then. But it was the best thing—when I gave birth to you it was the most wonderful thing I had known, I fell in love so to say, for the first time. And when I nursed you also it was like that—a passion. He was jealous, of course, in his passive way, he withdrew. And you—you were a difficult child, you cried all the time, you demanded my constant attention. I believe that every family has, a Sorgenkind, a worry child, and it is often the first one. And you, you were my Sorgenkind.

STRUWWELPETER, DAVY COHEN, AND THE JEWS

WHEN I WAS VERY YOUNG AND WE HAD JUST MOVED TO THAT TOWN, THERE WERE PIECES I TRIED TO sort out but could not. There was my parents' accent, for example, which I couldn't hear but had to believe existed, because it was the first thing anyone ever said when they met them. Sometimes they asked, "Have you been here long?," as if they were tourists from another country. If someone from school called me up and my mother answered, they always asked who was that lady with the funny accent. I only knew two other kids who had parents with accents: Beryl Wong, who was Chinese, so everyone expected her parents to talk funny, and Danny Cramer, who was the smallest boy in the whole grade, and our class clown, whom everyone treated like a pesty dog. Whenever I saw Danny's mother I was torn two ways. Her voice sounded familiar and warm to me, the right way for a mother's voice to sound, but she was bent and creased and walked with a limp, and the other kids called her a witch. Mrs. Cramer scared me by sounding like my mother and making me think I had to be like Danny Cramer.

My parents spoke German together sometimes. It was for telling secrets or talking to Oma and Opa on the phone. It was the sound of them talking in the living room when I fell asleep, as reassuring and benign as the hum of my mother's sewing machine. I don't think I connected the German with the inaudible accents.

Then there was being related to Sigmund Freud. He was the glowering man with a beard in the picture in the living room. When my mother wanted to promise something she would say, "I swear it on the beard of my grandfather." I thought that was a joke, just something funny to say, but I wasn't quite sure. Sigmund Freud was a famous man, I knew that. He was a genius, and being related to him was supposed to be a good thing, but for me it was all mixed up with the accent, and the third thing, which was being Jewish.

You said Jewish, never Jew, if you said it at all, which we almost never did. It had to do with my parents' accents, and with why we lived in a development, not an old house like my friend Sidney's and most of the other kids in my class. My parents had escaped, but almost everyone they knew had been caught and put on trains and taken to concentration camps where they were burnt up in big gas ovens. The Nazis tricked the Jews into going in the ovens by telling them they were showers and giving them fake bars of soap. Just as they felt the soap and realized it was really a block of wood, the Nazis turned on the gas. They picked up the wooden soap later, and used it on the next people. Some of the people my parents knew had been made into glue, and others had their skin peeled off and used for lamps. I used to be afraid of finding one of those lamps that had slipped by. I knew exactly how it would look: like snake or lizard skin, but a transparent pink color, pretty, like parchment. My father had escaped from one of these camps, but not such a bad one, a good one, he said, where people only starved to death, and afterwards he had hidden in the fields and eaten raw potatoes. The Nazis had tried to catch my mother and her mother and put them in a camp too, but they escaped on their bikes. The Nazis were right behind them, but they rode too fast for them and got away.

When I was six or seven I was terrified of the story of Hansel and Gretel, especially the part where the witch tries to stick Hansel in the oven. I pictured Mrs. Cramer as the witch, and the oven was a smaller version of the concentration camp ones. I always felt relieved when Gretel changed it around by pushing the witch in instead of Hansel, but I still didn't like the story.

I used to dream a lot about being fooled, about adults who smiled and gave you a bar of soap or a present and all the time were planning to cook you in an oven and then turn you into glue or a lamp. The Germans had done it to children too, I knew that. I was a suspicious child, as I am still a suspicious adult, and watchful.

Hansel and Gretel wasn't as bad as Struwwelpeter though. The cover had a boy with an orange shirt, green tights, bright frizzy yellow hair, and long, dirty fingernails, like claws. He was Struwwelpeter, and I could tell he was a Jew because his hair stuck straight out from his head like mine did if I didn't brush it down. I hated him and I hated the book, which was in German, and was about terrible things that happened to children. One little girl played with matches and her cats told her *Miau Miau Miau, DON'T play with matches,* but she did, and in the end she was burned to a crisp and the cats cried fake crocodile tears over her hair ribbon which was all that was left of her. Another boy sucked his thumb and a horrible little man came and cut off the ends of his fingers with a huge pair of scissors and the blood made a pool on the floor. But neither of these was as bad as the one about the little girl who starved to death. She said *I won't no I won't eat my soup,* and in every picture she got smaller and thinner until finally she was just bones, with the blue smocklike dress she had filled all the way up in the first picture hanging off her. In the last picture there was only a tombstone that said *This is the tomb of a child who would not eat.*

Did my mother read Struwwelpeter to me in German or

English? I remember the sound of the German, but I couldn't understand German and I understood those stories. Maybe she translated for me the first time and after that I understood. But why did she read those awful stories to me to begin with? I hated to see that book come out of the bookcase, and I hated the smell of it, which I was sure was a German smell, yellow and acrid. I thought it was the smell of concentration camps and ovens, and I thought I knew why the book smelled like that: it was held together by German glue, glue made of people. The little girl in the picture was me, being punished for not eating and for disappointing my mother, and it was the Jews, starving to death in the good concentration camps. I remember my mother's voice saying *Miau Miau Miau* for the cats, in German, giving me a warning.

Besides Danny Cramer, who didn't really count because his father was American and Protestant and their whole family went to the town's Unitarian church, the only other Jew in my class was Davy Cohen—and he didn't come till later, not until the fifth grade when I was ten. Davy Cohen was the ugliest boy I had ever seen. He had an adam's apple that stuck out, and a hooked nose, and hair that I could tell was even fuzzier than mine, which he kept cut very short and close to his head so no one could make fun of him or tell him it was dirty. It didn't take long for everyone to find out that Davy Cohen was smart. He was only about the tenth smartest in the class in English and History and French, but the third smartest in Math and Science—after Elizabeth Carlson and Susan Doralski, who were both sort of geniuses but had no friends and were weird. Davy Cohen wasn't especially weird, and he was even pretty good at sports. When we did geography in the sixth grade it turned out that he was the best of anyone at the things I was the very worst at: making charts and maps. Mrs. O'Leary, our seventh-grade English teacher who hated me, and who made me take my notebook home to recopy and organize six times until finally my mother did it for me, couldn't make Davy Cohen redo his notebook even once, even though she probably wanted to, because of his mother's complaints. Davy Cohen's notebook was perfect—as neat as any grownup's, with headings in different colors, outlines in roman numerals just the way Mrs. O'Leary had shown us, and every single thing organized alphabetically.

If Mrs. O'Leary couldn't show her true feelings about Davy Cohen, Mrs. Antler, the art teacher, could and did. Just like me, Mrs. Antler seemed to hate Davy Cohen instinctively from the first time she saw him, and she taunted him in front of everyone.

"So you think you're special, Mr. Cohen?" she'd say. "I can see you're much too advanced to take my humble suggestions. Maybe you think you should be teaching this class yourself? Your attitude may be catching," Mrs. Antler told Davy Cohen in the beginning of sixth grade. "I don't want you influencing the others." Then she sent him to sit at a table by himself.

All of us girls laughed at stuck-up, ugly Davy Cohen, sitting at a table in the corner by himself while the rest of us sat in groups of four or five, but it still made me feel funny. Teachers weren't supposed to go out of their way like that. I didn't say out loud to myself that Davy Cohen was a Jew and I was a Jew, but I wished Mrs. Antler would stop.

What made it more complicated was that almost as much as she hated Davy Cohen, Mrs. Antler loved me. Even though I was one of the least artistically talented of all the children in our class, I was her pet. Luckily, no one hated me for this because it was only Art, and anyway, everyone knew that Mrs. O'Leary picked on me, so it came out even in the end. One time Mrs. Antler framed and displayed a painting I did of a dog fight, which I knew myself was no good. The dogs didn't look like dogs, their faces were more like people's faces, and the blood from the fight had run all over the paper. She said it was great, though, because it had feelings in it. Davy Cohen's pictures were of real things. He did plane battles and racing cars and motorcycles and an occasional dinosaur, the same things all the boys drew, but his were better—he knew about proportion and everything he drew looked real. Since Mrs. Antler didn't let us use graph paper, he took out his ruler and made lines on his paper before he started to draw, and he always sketched his drawings in pencil first, which is another thing we weren't allowed to do, and which I could live with very happily. I would have loved art class, with its lovely huge sheets of blank white paper, its little tubs of all colors of paint, its big soft brushes, and the rare freedom I was allowed there to be my own messy self, but there was always the specter of Davy Cohen sitting alone at his special table in the corner. It made a bad feeling in my favorite class of the week, and I hated Davy Cohen for it.

I wonder now if it was his refusal to do things her way that infuriated Mrs. Antler, or what I concluded then, though I never said it, neither silently to myself nor out loud—that he was a Jew, an ugly Jew with a hooked nose. I want it to be the first, but why do I still care so much? What does it matter to me? Maybe it matters because Mrs. Antler was so nice to me—so nice that even now I love to paint and always find my own creations beautiful, no matter what anyone else thinks.

Mrs. Cohen came in to school to talk to Mrs. Antler about the way she was treating Davy. She came in all the time to complain to the teachers and to the principal, Mr. Lorrimer, about prayers and Christmas carols. When Mrs. O'Leary made us learn the Quality of Mercy Speech—in which Portia tries to persuade the bloodthirsty Jew, Shylock, to give up the pound of flesh he has coming to him—for the end-of-the-year assembly, she came in to complain about that. The next day Mrs. O'Leary told us that because of Some People who always wanted special treatment, we would have to take the phrase *Therefore, Jew* out of the speech, which, as she hoped we realized, was tampering with Shakespeare's Great Words. Because we had recited it every day for the past six weeks, in the assembly we all said, "Therefore, J—," and everyone snickered.

Mrs. Cohen was an American who spoke without an accent. She was a large, pale woman with thick black hair, Davy's hooked nose, and an angry expression on her face, and I hated her as much as I hated him. After she had been to school the teachers would not only treat Davy strangely, they would treat me the same way. I loved Christmas carols and knew at least two verses of all of them, so I almost cried when Mrs. O'Leary told me that Davy and I would be excused during the singing. It wasn't fair, it wasn't my mother who had made a fuss: she never would have, she knew better.

After his mother came in to talk to her, Mrs. Antler was even meaner to Davy Cohen than before, but he never cried or talked back when she tormented him. He just blushed and looked down at his paper with its drawing of two perfect battleships exchanging fire on a wild sea.

In high school, Davy Cohen's mother stopped coming in. He was co-captain of the tennis team with the class president, Bill Adams, and hung around with the top boys. Girls started saying that he wasn't so bad after all, and Sal Winter said yes when he asked her to the Junior Prom. I envied her for going to the prom, but the idea of dancing close with Davy Cohen almost made me sick. It was the same way I used to feel when I would glance over at him by accident and see him sitting there, alone at his special table in the corner, his neck bright red, a stubborn wooden expression on his face as he sketched out his drawings in pencil, all through the three years of art class with Mrs. Antler: sixth, seventh, and eighth grades.

HORSE GIRLS

I PLEDGE ALLEGIANCE TOTHEFLAG. OF THE UNITEDSTATESOFAMERICA. AND TO THE REPUBLIC. FOR whichitstands. One Nation. Under God. Indivisible. With liberty. And justice. For all.

"You may sit down now," Kai St. Clair told us. We took our hands off our hearts, sat down, folded our hands on our desks, and began, *Our fatherwhoartin heaven, hallowed be thy name.* Even though it was the first day back to school, Kai knew exactly what to do from last year. After we finished the Lord's Prayer, she opened our class bible and announced, "Psalm 23." As she began to read *The Lord is my shepherd, I shall not want,* we could hear a roar as the Lord's Prayer began in 3C and 3B, the two middle groups whose rooms were on either side of us. At almost the same time, the Pledgeofallegiance started up faintly from 3A, the lowest group, whose room was next to the central corridor so the principal could step in easily when they got out of hand. Just like last year, in second grade, our top group started and finished first, and 3A was last, even though their teacher read their psalm to them. As Kai tossed her hair back, smiled sweetly, and ended, *Surely goodness and mercy shall follow me all the days of my life,* we could hear *libertyan justice forall* echoing down the hall. "Very nice, Kai," Miss Blanchard told her. "You may take your seat. Bill Adams, I'd like you to lead the opening exercises tomorrow morning."

Looking over the familiar faces in the room, I felt relieved. This time last year I had been a scared new girl, and the others had been a blur. Now I knew everyone in our class by name, and most of the others in the school by sight, and I understood just where each one fit in the hierarchy in which the world was arranged.

Our new teacher, Miss Blanchard, had done just right to choose Kai St. Clair and Bill Adams. I was sure that Kai had never been scared of anything in her whole life. We had elected her vice-president of our class last year, and Bill president. As far as I could tell, class officers didn't do anything special. The elections were just a way to show who were the top kids, and because our class was the best, our elections showed who were the top kids in the whole school. This year we were called 3D and the worst group was 3A, and last year we had been the hummingbirds and the worst group had been the eagles, but grownups had to be pretty stupid if they thought that fooled anybody.

Kai St. Clair always played with the other horse girls— Biscuit Thorne, Lizbeth Standish, and Caro Warner—at recess. The horse girls had golden or very light brown hair, held back with plastic barrettes, and they talked about the private schools some of them were going to when they got older, and the real horses they had at home. At school they had hard plastic horses which they exercised decorously on the steps near the door, making horse noises: whinnies, snorts, and neighs. I must have thought they were awarded those horses at birth, because I was amazed to see them on display just like ordinary toys when my mother and I went to the Country Store, where the horse girls' mothers bought them their Fair Isle sweaters, plaid wool skirts, and penny loafers. We were there to look at the pattern on one of the sweaters so my mother could copy it in the one she was going to knit for me. I knew it wouldn't come out the same as theirs, but that was only right. I paused reverently for a long time in front of the shelf where the horses stood and carefully reached out to stroke my favorite—a white one with a black mane and black spots on its flank. "Would you like one, Schnuckie?," my mother asked me, but although, as she often told me, I was a needy child who wanted everything, I shook my head. Those horses were reserved for the horse girls. I knew they were not meant for me.

Some of the horse girls and some of the top boys did disappear after fourth or fifth grade, and I never saw them again. My sort of friend and rival, Sal Winter, who went to the dances the country club had for kids at Christmas and in the summer, reported seeing them there, though. Sal's mother played tennis with Caro's mother, and Sal said her mother said Caro's mother said Caro was at Miss Smythe's, and that her horse had gone with her and was boarding in a special stable they had for them, which was lucky because Caro and her horse were inseparable. Those horse girls who didn't go to private school let it be known that they were still with us because their parents believed in giving public schooling a try.

"Dad's going to let me stay right through high school if I keep up my grades," Biscuit Thorne told some of us. "He said Radcliffe was soon enough for all that sort of thing." Biscuit Thorne, who had long honey-colored hair and blue eyes, always got picked right away in dancing school, but so did Kai St. Clair, even though by that time she was taller than all the boys and had the bad kind of braces, the kind that totally covered your teeth with silver wires, instead of the more moderate kind with one band of wire, like Sidney and Sal and I had. Kai's father and Sidney's father were the same kind of professors at different universities so they knew each other, and sometimes the two families had dinner together, and afterwards Sidney's mother would talk about Kai's perfect manners. Sidney hated those dinners. She always said Kai St. Clair was going to wake up one day and find that she had turned into a horse because she whinnied too much.

"What delicious cake, Mrs. de Toqueville, neigh neigh. I will have some more if you don't mind, neigh neigh." Sidney imitated Biscuit's perfect manners. I knew Sidney could have been a horse girl herself if she'd wanted to. Her parents talked the same way as all the horse girls' parents did, in clipped tones, high up in their throats, as if part of their air was getting cut off. Every summer Sidney was invited to swim in the St. Clair's pool, but even in third grade she thought plastic horses were stupid, and later on she despised any kid who ran for student council, which, she told me, was a complete waste of time and only decided stupid things like if the school dance was going to have Hawaiian Nights or Paris in the Rain for its theme.

The horse girls were always elected to student council. Besides being vice-president of everything, they sang in the select chorus, played field hockey, lacrosse, and tennis, and although, with Elizabeth Carlson and Susan Doralski around, they couldn't be the very best in any subject, they never got any marks but *A*'s and *B*'s. They had pajama parties at each other's houses, which were all old, and in the summer they went to Maine or Martha's Vineyard or to islands with names that no one had ever heard of because they were private ones, not on the map.

Sidney's house was old, too, and when I went over there in winter I learned to wear an extra sweater because it was freezing. After I got home from dinner there, I sometimes went in the icebox for a second meal of corned beef and pickles, or cold chicken and potato chips. And Sidney only had two dresses, both of them hand-me-downs from her cousin. Still, I knew the de Toquevilles were better than us.

"You live in a development," Patsy Prudhomme had explained when she came over on her bike to play with me the summer we moved to that town. "My dad said we don't want developments here—all kinds of people will move in." I'd been excited to see her, a skinny little girl with dark red hair cut in ragged bangs and bright golden eyes like a cat's, wearing patched dungarees and holding an old bike with fat tires and back-pedal brakes, when she knocked on our door the first time. "I heard there was a new girl here," she said to my mother. "Can I come in and play with her?" I'd never known any kids who went places on their own, without a grownup. After a few weeks, though, my mother wouldn't let Patsy in because she broke something every time she came. I hated going to her house because of her fierce big brother who'd had polio and walked with a crutch, and who would reach out and pretend to hit me with it when I walked by, and because you always had to be quiet since her father, who had something secret wrong with him, had to lie down a lot. Sometimes he would get up unexpectedly and start shouting at everyone for making too much noise. Patsy only liked to play scary games, like sliding in trays down the steep hill which came out on the main road, or seeing who could ride bikes longest with no hands or with a blindfold on. When school started in the fall she told everyone I was a scared baby who lived in a development, and when I made friends with her best friend, Sidney, we became enemies for life.

Patsy, Sal Winter, and most of the other kids in our top class went to the Unitarian church in town, but Sidney and most of the horse girls had to go to another town for church because they were High Episcopalians, a religion you could tell just from its name was the best. The High Episcopalians, Sidney told me, would never have invited my family to join the very same week we moved in, the way the Unitarians had: you could only be a High Episcopalian if you were born one. Sidney told me her church was one of the oldest in America and that her family had always been High Episcopalians. In the picture of it I had in my head, Sidney's church had red velvet and incense, huge white candles as thick and tall as a child, and pews that locked and had different families' names engraved on the doors. I could have told Sidney that my family had always been Jews, but somehow I knew it was not the same thing.

Once or twice I went along on their ski weekends as a guest, but I never actually joined the Pilgrim Fellowship, the youth group of the Unitarian church, even though their day trips to prisons and mental hospitals, and to the nearby city's Black

ghetto, were just my sort of thing. There was something about
the smile on the face of the minister who came to our house
to invite us to join that made me uncomfortable. "We are a
church which welcomes everyone," he told my mother, smiling at himself like that was something really special.

If, as Patsy Prudhomme had told me, our new house in the
woods, warm and light as it was, with one whole wall nothing
but windows, was inferior to the cold, old houses of the top
kids, everyone knew it was *much* better than the junky little
houses of the kids in the lowest group who lived near the rail-
road tracks, or by the highway, and went to St. Mary's Church.
Those Catholic kids had fathers who drove the town garbage
truck and the snow plow, or worked at the town dump, and
some of their mothers packed groceries at Fred's Variety, the
only store in town where my mother never shopped because
she said the prices were ridiculous. There was Rocky Balducci,
who was triple-jointed and looked like he was made of rubber,
and who hated me as much as I hated him because the boys in
my class would sometimes gang up at recess, grab him by both
arms and legs, and heave him in my direction, screaming, "Cootie
zone, cootie zone!" There was Maria deSalvo, who wore heavy
pancake make-up and teased her hair in the fifth grade; her best
friend Betty Leone, who wore a grownup-sized bra in the fourth;
and her brother Eddie Leone, who should have been in junior
high only he could never learn to read and so kept being left
back. Then there was Mary Riley, who everyone said smelled,
whose mother cleaned Sal Winter's house twice a week, and
who wore Sal's old clothes to school, only we were supposed
to pretend not to notice when she had them on. We only heard
about Betty's bra and Eddie's problem with reading thirdhand
from Mrs. Riley, because we never saw the kids in the dumbest
class except sometimes on the school bus. We did have recess
together, but each group had its own corner of the playground.

How did I, who, as my mother told me later on, had a low-
average IQ because I had failed to put even two pieces of the
Black Beauty puzzle together; who had not managed to arrange
the blocks into any pattern at all, let alone the one in the pic-

ture; who only learned to read in the middle of the second grade; and who never did figure out things like telling time, or right and left—how did I make it into the top group when we first moved to town? I am sure now that my mother must have gone in to school and arranged it, kissing the principal's feet, employing all of her foreign, social worker's charm on him, and swearing on the beard of her famous grandfather that she would work with me every night until I caught up.

It didn't occur to me then that any arranging might have been necessary. I, like all the others in our class, assumed, at least at first, that my membership in the top group was as much a part of me as my brown eyes. The fact that I understood only half of what went on in school was irrelevant. I belonged in the smartest group because I was smart, just as surely as the Cheap Girls, Betty and Maria, who spent recess trying on their big sisters' lipstick, and chasing Eddie, Rocky, and Steve Palooka around the cement part of the playground, belonged in the worst group because they were dumb.

In all my years at that school I knew only one person who ever questioned this assumption, and although that person, Elizabeth Carlson, was the smartest one in our class, she was also one of the wierdest, and no one took her questions very seriously. Elizabeth might have been the smartest girl in the top class, which made her the smartest kid in the whole grade, but her position was much lower than mine, which was considerably enhanced by my friendship with Sidney. Elizabeth wanted badly to be my friend, and from the time Sidney and I started the Philosophy Club in the third grade, she had invited me to her house all the time.

The idea for the Philosophy Club, like the idea for our favorite game later on, Mental Hospital, came from one of my mother's thick psychology books. There was a chapter called "The Moral Development of Children" which had a series of little stories with attached questions which you could ask children to find out what stage of moral development they had reached. Once Sidney and I had asked each other all the questions in the book, we started to make up our own. Pretty soon, we could always predict each other's answers, which was boring, so, as we did from time to time when we felt the need, we formed a club. The Philosophy Club lasted only a few months, but during that time, Sal Winter, Patsy Prudhomme, Sidney, Elizabeth Carlson, and I met every noon recess in the roomy shadow of a certain big tree and, sitting in a sedate circle, gently debated matters of morality. Was it O.K. to steal if you were starving? Was killing wrong if there was a war? If your parents beat you with a stick, was it disloyal to tell the police on them? If you caught your best friend cheating on a test, should you tell on her? If someone gave you the choice of saving your own mother by killing ten other people you'd never met, what should you do? Elizabeth Carlson passionately loved the Philosophy Club and wanted it to continue long after the rest of us lost interest, even though she sometimes got overinvolved in the debate, becoming furious, then white-faced and tearful when someone disagreed with her, so that Sidney had to tell her to go away and come back when she had calmed down.

In addition to this fatal lack of detachment, the way Elizabeth looked kept her firmly on the bottom of our class's social ladder. Sidney's dresses were not new, but at least they fit her round frame. Elizabeth Carlson's dresses and her blue jumpers looked to me as though they had belonged, not to her older sister or her cousin, but to her grandmother. Elizabeth, who had attained almost her full growth by the fourth grade, and who towered above the rest of us until high school when she was suddenly only average height, belted these long, straight, shroudlike garments around her waist, shortening the skirt by pulling folds of material over the red plastic belt. At a time when a meal without meat was not a real meal, Elizabeth Carlson was a vegetarian, whom you could never invite for dinner, and who even refused to wear leather. Instead of acceptable brown leather shoes, which ranged from the horse girls' fashionable penny loafers to my own buckled shoes to Sidney's worn and scuffed lace-ups, Elizabeth wore her smelly white gym sneakers to school, even more glaringly out of place when paired with those long jumpers and dresses. Elizabeth's glasses looked like hand-me-downs from her grandmother too. They were very thick and had light blue frames with wings and fake pearls in them. If she fell down or took off her glasses to wipe them, she looked young and lost, and it was possible to see her very blue eyes.

No one ever called Elizabeth Carlson Liz or Lizbeth, like Lizbeth Standish. Instead she was referred to by her whole name—Elizabeth Carlson. Only gentle, boring Jennifer Thomas and occasionally Sidney and I really talked to her. But no one mocked Elizabeth Carlson either, or thrust Rocky Balducci at her at recess. I think this was not because the other kids were in awe of her intelligence, as they might well have been, but rather because no one, adult or child, was prepared to deal with what Sidney and I called Elizabeth Carlson's fits. These outbursts, which even the meanest boys like Brian Moody and Charlie Nichols found it hard to enjoy, usually occurred early in the year. Elizabeth always got *A*'s, and we had long ago accepted that in everything but Math, where Susan Doralski occasionally did better, she was the smartest. Sometimes, however, a new teacher, who did not yet understand things, decided that it would be good for someone else to come out on top, and ignored her or altered her scores just a little.

It must have been raining hard that day in the first few weeks of fourth grade because Mrs. Freeman kept us in for recess and organized us into two teams to play a game. It turned out to be a math lesson in disguise, which involved coming up with quick answers to word problems and waving your hand to be recognized. When you got it right, your team scored a point. It was the kind of game without turns where someone like me could sit back and watch, so I wasn't worried for myself, only uneasy for Elizabeth. Her need to be best always got out of hand when she felt that a whole team depended on her performance, and her feelings had a way of invading me, so that during her outbursts I would blush deeply and feel my scalp begin to itch in a kind of sympathetic agony of embarrassment. Midway into the game, which had quickly disintegrated into the usual boring match between Elizabeth and Susan Doralski, Mrs. Freeman asked a question, and Danny Cramer suddenly shouted in triumph and raised his hand. Math was Danny's best subject, but he never came in first, and Mrs. Freeman must have felt herself perfectly justified in ignoring Elizabeth's wildly waving hand and calling on him. The game progressed, but Elizabeth was no longer playing. From the back of the room, I could see her face turn white as Susan Doralski complacently chalked up points for the other side.

"Mrs. Freeman, I think you forgot to call on Elizabeth," Jennifer Thomas interrupted the game urgently. "A while back. Her hand was up before Danny's."

"Never mind!" Mrs. Freeman was cheery and brisk, either oblivious or determined to brave the storm. "You let me worry about that, Jennifer, and try to come up with some answers yourself. Anyway, it's just a game!"

"DON'T EVER SAY THAT!" Elizabeth's voice, exceptionally deep and gravelly for a nine-year-old's, rent the tense silence. "I CAN'T STAND IT WHEN PEOPLE SAY THAT! IT DOESN'T MATTER IF IT'S A GAME. YOU KNEW I HAD MY HAND UP FIRST AND YOU DIDN'T CALL ON ME!" Elizabeth's tremendous effort not to cry had turned her from white to purple, and her whole body was visibly trembling. "IT'S NOT FAIR!" she shouted, exploding into rending sobs as she scraped her chair back and ran for the girl's room. "CAN'T YOU SEE? IT'S NOT JUST!"

Looking back, I can see that this was the difference between Elizabeth Carlson and the rest of us. Smart as she was, she lacked the saving cynicism that allowed us to go through the motions and get on with it. She kept expecting that adults would be fair; that if you knew the answer first you would be called on; and even that the many stupid things adults made us do, like saying the Lord's Prayer and the Pledgeofallegiance, were actually supposed to mean something. This, along with her compelling need to be best, made her life an endless struggle. Sidney and I, who prided ourselves on our understanding of human nature, never tired of discussing Elizabeth's peculiar psychology. Most of our discussions centered on her parents, who, she had told everyone, used to be Catholic missionaries in Africa until they lost their faith, and on the white, lacy First Communion dress that hung in a special place in her closet.

When I heard Elizabeth Carlson's creaky voice on the phone I always had a sinking feeling. She made no small talk, which would have given me time to come up with an excuse, but instead got straight to the point. "Hello, Rachel, this is Elizabeth Carlson," she always explained lugubriously, as if it could have been anyone else. "Can you come over?" I allowed myself to say no to Elizabeth four times out of five, but by the fifth time I usually gave in to the raw hurt in her voice and said yes.

The first thing you had to do when you went over to Elizabeth's house was go upstairs to her bare room and look at the communion dress. "I never know what I'm supposed to say about it," I complained to Sidney. "When I say, 'It's pretty,' she just looks mad."

"I try to look serious and nod," Sidney explained. "It's something religious." After a viewing of the communion dress, Elizabeth usually wanted to play Monopoly, which was the longest, most boring game in the world. I was generally skillful at making other kids believe they wanted to play what I wanted, but my subtle persuasions didn't stand a chance against the force of Elizabeth's need. It was easier just to play Monopoly and vow to myself that I would never come again. Anxious for it to be over so I could go home, I always spent my money right away, buying up all the expensive hotels and houses I could find. This was a tactic which could backfire, though, and then Elizabeth would go white and red and tremble with the effort to be a good loser, while the tears stood in her eyes.

In the beginning of fifth grade, Sidney and I rolled our eyes at each other when, instead of standing with the rest of us as we saluted the flag, Elizabeth Carlson stayed firmly in her seat.

"What's the matter, Elizabeth?" our pretty new teacher Mrs. Neal asked her after opening exercises were over. "Aren't you feeling well?"

"I've decided that I can't salute the flag any more," Eliz-

abeth answered in her hollow tones. "I thought about it all summer and I don't think it's right." Mrs. Neal looked perplexed.

"Not *right?* Why is that?"

"You see, I can't really pledge my allegiance to a flag, or
to a country," Elizabeth explained. "The only allegiance I can
have is to what I believe in. What if the law of the country told
me to go in the army and shoot people? I couldn't obey, because
I'm a pacifist. So I can't salute the flag." The whole class giggled, glad of the interruption in the morning ritual. Everyone
knew girls didn't have to go in the army anyway.

Eh-e-e-e. Brian Moody did that sputtering noise boys made
for shooting. "Shoot some communists, Elizabeth. You're in the
army now." *Eh-e-e-e.* Charlie Nichols and Chester Laughton
joined in.

"Also," Elizabeth continued, ignoring them, "it says *liberty
and justice for all.* And there isn't. Negroes don't have justice.
They have to live in the ghetto. Daddy took me there over the
summer, and they have garbage all over the streets, and babies
get bitten by rats. It's not fair. And even right here in this
school—"

"I can see you've thought very hard about this, Elizabeth,"
Mrs. Neal interrupted her. "How about if you just stand and
mouth the words if it doesn't feel right to you to speak them
out loud."

"NO!" Elizabeth was getting red. "THAT WOULD BE HYP-
OCRITICAL." *Let it go, let it go,* I telegraphed silently to Mrs.
Neal. She met my eyes and nodded in understanding. All the
next week, Elizabeth sat silent and polite in her seat as we saluted
the flag, then joined us eagerly in prayer. The calm was shat-
tered, though, when Mr. Lorrimer, our principal, made a surprise visit to our class one afternoon. After asking Mrs. Neal's
permission, he addressed us from the front of the room, his
long, jowly face drooping solemnly like a basset hound's the
same way it had when he came in to tell us that Merit Stone had
tried to burn down the gym over the weekend and would never
again be welcome on the grounds of our school.

"I have received a report from one of our parent representatives," he said. "He told me that a student in this fifth-grade class is refusing to obey the law of the land. You children in 5D have a special responsibility, you know. The children in the other groups look up to you for an example. So I was especially disappointed to hear that it was someone from this room!"

"It was me!" Elizabeth stood up proudly, and Mr. Lorrimer shook his head, faking surprise. "A smart girl like you, Elizabeth Carlson! A girl who should know better." He took her to his office for a little talk, but as any of us could have told him, this only hardened her resistance. Then he called her parents in, but they supported her in her stance. In the end, Elizabeth Carlson was expelled for three whole days, a worse punishment than Charlie Nichols got when he released the science room's boa constrictor in the heating system, or that Brian Moody got when he pushed Danny Cramer down on the concrete playground and broke his arm. When she returned, holding her head up proudly, she was exiled to the tiny cloakroom in the back of the classroom until opening exercises were over. We could hear her hollow tones booming out from there during the Lord's Prayer. As far as I know, she never saluted the flag again.

By the time my little brother was in junior high school, saluting the flag was no longer compulsory, and all that praying had been replaced by a moment of silence. But at that time and in that place I did not understand what on earth, except maybe the desire to martyr herself, could motivate Elizabeth Carlson to make such a fuss about something as stupid as the Pledgeofallegiance.

In sixth grade I served a bitter year of exile in the second-to-top group and lost track of Elizabeth Carlson. Then, in the seventh grade, we moved from the smaller one-story red brick elementary school building to the longer and newer junior high school, with its modern wood panels set in red brick. Here we rotated into different teachers' rooms for different subjects, and a few kids were allowed to be smart in some subjects and dumb in others. I was reunited with my top group for English, History, Science, Art, and Music, but for Math I was sent to the second to lowest group, and Elizabeth Carlson, Susan Doralski,

Merrill Stone, Jerry Nails, Davy Cohen, and Danny Cramer were selected to attend a class for math geniuses taught at the local university. They had a special bus to take them into town and got to miss a whole afternoon twice a week. For Homeroom, Gym, Beginning Typing, and Home Ec., we were placed in what they called Mixed Ability Groups, where, natural enemies, we snarled at each other from separate sections of the room. Those cheap girls fulfilled my worst expectations. They were not only stupid, I decided, they were also mean and tough. They slashed at my feet with hockey sticks even when I was on their team, shouted so loudly in my ear that I got more confused than I already was and threw the basketball at the wrong basket, and left little notes stuck on my notebook with bubblegum with messages like, *Cooty Christ Killer* and *Just wait till gym we will get you.* This continued until Sidney caught Betty Leone writing *Cootys* on my gym suit in red lipstick. She grabbed Betty and shoved her in the shower with her slip on, and when she tried to come out, Sidney smacked her until she cried and told her to spread the word that the same thing would happen to anyone who messed with me again.

In the end, I turned out to be the very worst in all the classes I had with the cheap girls: Gym, Math, Typing, and especially Home Ec. Cooking was O.K., but no one had warned me that sewing was so much like map-making or putting a puzzle together. Maybe it was a comfort to those girls who had been stuck in the low classes all their lives to have one of the snobby top kids turn out to be so dumb. Whatever the reason, Maria DeSalvo and Betty Leone both made fudge for the party that Mrs. Visconti, our Home Ec. teacher, held when I finished my skirt. Mrs. Visconti had dyed blonde hair, long red nails, and matching scarlet lipstick. She was the only one of our teachers who liked the cheap girls best, and we were pretty sure she had been one herself when she was young. Mrs. Visconti disapproved of Sidney and me before she even knew us because once, when we were in the fourth grade and had been playing explorers in the woods behind my house, we had come upon a bulldozer which said *Visconti Bulldozers* on it. We climbed up and were pretending to drive it off when a man came racing out of the woods and started shouting at us that the bulldozers were private property, and we better tell him our names so the police could send us to jail. We told him our names and ran off laughing at him, since everybody knew the police didn't send you to jail. You had to have a trial, and anyway, our parents wouldn't let them take us away. The next day Mrs. Visconti came into our fourth-grade classroom and told Sidney and me that if she ever heard we had interfered with her husband's property again, she would personally see to it that we failed Home Ec. in junior high. ''You kids really think you own everything, don't you?'' she said.

It didn't take much of a grudge on Mrs. Visconti's part to make me almost fail Home Ec. in seventh grade. While the cheap girls made themselves skirts, dresses, and even fancy suits with jackets and matching mini-skirts, and everyone else managed at least a skirt, a jumper, and a sun dress, I worked and worked at my shiny orange mini-skirt all year long. Nobody but Sidney knew that I finally snuck that skirt home and my mother finished it for me. She ripped out what I had done and did it over, but then we both realized that it looked too good, so she had to rip it out a second time and do it again, more like I might have done if I had understood anything about patterns. When I brought in the chewed-up looking skirt, Mrs. Visconti let the whole class have a party. She must have been convinced that I had tried because she gave me a *D,* not an *F.* I wore my orange mini-skirt to school once. It was so short I was sure the straps of my garter belt must be showing, so I hung it in my closet where it stayed until I put it in the Good Will box when I left for college.

As for Elizabeth Carlson, she was as smart in Home Ec. as in everything else, but she refused to go to the math class for geniuses. She said it was unfair. Why should *she* get to go somewhere special twice a week and not the kids in the lower classes who needed the chance more? In high school, when all the top kids from the top classes in the three towns which made up the regional high school were selected for honors classes, she refused to join them too, even though everyone said that only the honors kids would get into good colleges. I was taking honors French and History and English, and so I didn't see as much of Elizabeth, but we did work on the literary magazine together. She was as smart as ever, and had kept Jennifer Thomas, whom she said laughed her out of her moods, as her friend. She had even learned how to laugh at herself. She had taken advanced Home Ec. with all the cheap girls, but instead of sewing herself some clothes, she sewed costumes for the school plays. I told her I thought she was being inconsistent since only horse girls and top boys ever got picked for parts in the plays. I tried out every year and never once got in, even though everyone knew that I was a much better actress than Caro Warner, who usually played the heroine. Elizabeth looked worried and thanked me for reminding her of this. She said she would be sorry to have to stop sewing for the plays, because she was thinking of going into sewing costumes in the theatre.

"I can't allow myself to do anything competitive," she said. "I just can't trust myself. You remember how I used to get?" I told Elizabeth how worried I was that I wouldn't get into a good college because of my *D*'s in Math and my low scores on the Math SAT's, and she said that even though she was a National Merit Finalist, she thought she probably wouldn't go to college at all because not everyone had the opportunity and going would be participating in the unfair class system of this country.

I told my mother about it, and she was shocked. "It's tragic. I can't believe it, a girl of such ability throwing away her life," she said. "I can't bear even to think about it, it gives me heart-beat." *Heart-beat* was something my father usually had, not my mother, but these were the only words she could find for what she meant. "It's too awful, the smartest girl in the whole class," she kept saying. "She could go to Radcliffe, she could go anywhere. Her parents need their heads examined."

When we graduated from high school, it was the horse girls who went to Radcliffe. I went to a small private college no one from that town had heard of, where I starred in the plays, took drugs, and was generally very happy. Elizabeth Carlson got a job sewing costumes for a theater in New York.

Have a good life, she wrote in my yearbook, at the end of our senior year. *I will too. Or else go to the crazy house.*

BROWNIES

WHEN MY BROWNIE LEADER, MRS. SACRIN,
TALKED TO ME IN THE VOICE IT SEEMED TO ME THAT SHE
reserved for me—as sticky and sweet as rotting meat, reeking
with something secret and hateful—it sent a wave of discom-
fort all through me, the way the ruff on the back of our dog
Dusty's neck stood up when she was following me on my bike
and we had to pass the fierce dogs in Kate's Farm Lane. My reaction was so clear and strong that it never occurred to me to question my perceptions about Mrs. Sacrin's feelings for me. What
I did speculate about was why she felt that mixture of disgust,
hatred, and pity I heard in her voice. Now I can remember Mrs.
Sacrin's daughter Mandy telling a group of assembled kids in
gory detail about how the Jews killed Christ. In those days,
though, my conclusions had nothing to do with Jews.

I joined the Brownies because my mother had figured out
that it was what American girls in that town did. She signed me

up for them the way she signed me up for dancing school three years later, so that I would fit in. Much later, when I was fourteen or so, she insisted I learn to dive, something I had no intention of doing.

"But that's how teenagers meet each other, at the diving board," she insisted, her voice frantic with the knowledge that boys avoided me. At fourteen I knew my mother could be wrong, and that diving lessons would not turn me into one of the horse girls like Lizbeth Standish or Biscuit Thorne, or even into my friends Sidney or Merrill. I wonder now if she had seen a movie or read a book that had diving in it as a key ingredient for popularity with boys, or whether she got her evidence from that summer when we still lived in the city but had sublet a house in the suburbs, complete with a membership to the town swimming pool, and she was too pregnant with my brother to do anything but sit and watch us swim and observe the action around the diving board. Even so, it seems to me she must have read the evidence backwards, changing it around to fit her own hatred of feminine passivity. Wouldn't it have been the boys who dived and the girls who watched and squealed when they got pushed in? I can picture them now in her version, slim, self-assured girls wearing flowered bathing caps, diving off the diving board and emerging under the admiring stares of crowds of boys. There is a float, they are drinking Pepsi, they are taking off their bathing caps and shaking out their straight blonde hair, they are arranging with the boys to go to the drive-in where they will kiss each other in the back seat.

In second grade, when I was seven, my mother was never wrong, and neither the weekly torment of Mrs. Sacrin nor the example of my friend Sidney, who had told her mother firmly that she had no interest in Brownies and had never joined, gave me the idea of quitting Brownies myself. For me, Brownies on Thursday afternoons seemed as inevitable as arithmetic or softball games in gym—something to dread and live through, not to question or avoid.

To be fair, it was not only my mother's decree which had influenced me to join the Brownies. I cherished great hopes for them in the beginning—and all because of the uniform. Even though going shopping for patterns and material with my mother was one of my favorite things to do, I had a private theory that part of my trouble was that she sewed my clothes. Then, as now, we were both drawn to a certain richness and extravagance of color and pattern, and we shopped for material the way we might have picked a bouquet of flowers in a rich Alpine meadow. We hated the brown and navy-blue pleated skirts topped with a white blouse and scrawny cardigan worn by most of the other girls. Skirts drooped off my skinny hips anyway, so we favored low- or high-waisted dresses, flowered, striped, or polka-dotted. We both had a weakness for pink and red, and for combinations of blue and green. When the dresses were finished they fit my skinny frame perfectly, instead of hanging on me the way store-bought clothes always did. One especially outstanding winter jumper, a long-time favorite of mine, was made of a nubby, furry material with large black, brown, yellow, and orange spots like a hyena's coat, and had, as its crowning glory, a furry spotted purse to match, with a zipper and a real leather handle.

Other mothers purred over my clothes and wondered aloud how mine found the time. "Doesn't she go out to work too?" they asked, clicking their tongues. "I don't know how she does it." Kids just stared.

I knew that the Brownie Uniform would be different, though. My mother and I had carefully written down my measurements on a special yellow form, just the same as everyone else's, and sent it in.

A few weeks later the uniform arrived in the mail like it was supposed to. It was a brown shirtwaist dress with brown plastic buttons down the front and a brown plastic-and-cloth belt. When I tried the dress on, it became obvious that Brownies were meant to be fatter than me. It was so loose that folds of fabric had to be gathered in by the plastic belt, which was much too long, so that my mother had to make special holes in it, and snip off the end. It still waved pitifully in the air, though. The rough cloth chapped my skin, and the material was so thin that in the winter it had to be worn with an undershirt underneath, and with the special Brownie sweater, an itchy dark-green acrylic cardigan, on top. There were even special Brownie socks, with raised horseshoes embroidered on the material, socks which were so slippery and metallic that they vanished inside my shoes as soon as I put them on, and remained there in a bunchy lump all day. When I looked in the mirror the first time I had every-thing on, my hopes that the Brownie uniform might transform me into someone just like everybody else were dashed. I could see at once that the uniform had the opposite effect: I looked not only different, but like the girl who *would not* eat her soup in the worst Struwwelpeter story—a girl you could tell there was something wrong with.

Because of this I was not that surprised at the tone of Mrs. Sacrin's voice when she spoke to me at our first meeting, Thurs-day after school in Mandy Sacrin's basement. Nor, as I had never been in Brownies before, did I question our activities. In Brown-ies we marched: left foot right foot, while Mrs. Sacrin chanted "Left left left my wife and thirty-eight kids right!" That was how they marched in the army, Mrs. Sacrin said, and that was what the men sang who had to leave their wives and children to go and fight for their country. We Brownies could help our coun-try too if there was a war. I knew about the war my parents had escaped from, which had concentration camps and ovens but no marching as far as I had been told. I had just finished a book about Abraham Lincoln, though, one of those orange biogra-phies which Sidney and I were reading one by one, and I knew the Civil War did have lots of marching. I tried to pretend that I was marching to free the slaves, but it was hard to do because Mrs. Sacrin didn't just let us march in peace. She kept shouting left and right. My mother had taught me that if I pretended I was picking up a pencil without thinking about it, the hand I reached for the pencil with would always be my right one. But you couldn't reach for a pencil while you were marching, and anyway, it was more difficult with feet. On top of left and right, there was knowing when to change them around. The other Brownies seemed in on the secret, but it was all a mystery to me. Soon the very mention of marching made my stomach hurt.

When one of the other kids stuck her leg out at the wrong time, Mrs. Sacrin would rap her on it and tell her to concentrate—didn't she want to help her country? She prided herself on being especially strict with her own daughter, Mandy, who turned out to be a perfect marcher, so that Mrs. Sacrin had to make up things to scold her for, like not holding her head up straight. But when I marched she looked at me, shook her head sadly, and asked me very gently, in that voice, to pretty please try my very best, just to please Mrs. Sacrin, dear. After a while she would pull me out of the line, holding me gingerly by a fold of my Brownie uniform with her long tan-colored nails, curved in at the ends, and tell me to help Mrs. Sacrin like a good girl, and pretend to be the audience at the parade, which was an important thing too, dear! Because if there's no audience who will clap for our loyal men?

After practicing marching in the basement of Mandy's house, we tried marching on the road in front of it. You were supposed to see a row of legs moving all together, and if one leg was out of step the Brownie troop could never earn its marching badge or dare to show itself in public and we would let down our country, and all because of one person. We were preparing for something big, along with all the other troops like ours. All of them were practicing marching like we were, and soon there would be a giant parade with every single Brownie troop coming together. If one person didn't know her right from left, she would spoil it for everyone.

It was better to hold my mouth in a smile and clap weakly every so often to keep Mrs. Sacrin from coming over and telling me again how important the audience was.

The other thing that Brownies had to do was tie knots: special ones that involved left and right again, and over and under, and a whole set of mystifying directions, and which, if they were done right, would never ever come undone, no matter what. If you had tied a boat up with one of those knots, and there was a hurricane, for instance, your boat would be safe. There were the granny and the half hitch and all kinds of other knots, but

I practiced the square knot over and over and never got it right, and Mrs. Sacrin said, "Oh dear, you do try so hard, honey. Never mind, will you help Mrs. Sacrin with the refreshments?"

I don't remember any particular kids in Brownies, though I assume some of the girls in my class at school must have been there. At Brownies they were only a tight bunch of good marchers and good knot-tyers, with myself on the outside, encased in my shame, being talked to by Mrs. Sacrin.

I don't think I ever told my mother about knots or marching. Mostly when I couldn't do something, like multiplication tables, or telling time, we practiced it over and over, but we never practiced Brownie things together, though we practiced right and left until the very mention of these terms could send me into a fog of stupidity. And I didn't complain to my mother about Mrs. Sacrin because it never occurred to me that there was anything to complain about. I knew it was not really my bad marching or lack of knot-tying skills that made her despise me. Those things were just an outward sign of who I really was. Mrs. Sacrin, it was obvious to me, had found out about Serena. Why else would she treat me like that?

SHAME

IN SERENA'S WAITING ROOM, THE YEAR I WAS
SIX, BEFORE WE MOVED FROM THE CITY TO THE TOWN,
there was a boy who ran around the room in circles handling
all the toys without really playing with them. He had a large,
white head which wobbled on his thin neck, and he talked all
the time in a strange high-pitched voice, saying the same things
over and over again, like when my *Peter and the Wolf* record
got stuck on the record player and said, "The little bird a—, the
little bird a—," until I scratched the needle ahead to make it go
on. I was afraid of that boy. I hated seeing him, but I had to, once
a week, and even at night in my dreams where he appeared as
a kind of nightmare Humpty Dumpty, forcing me to go down
with him where we both belonged, in the closed endless tunnel reserved for people who had something wrong with them.

"What do you do in there?" my mother asked me anx-
iously when I came out of the office. I shrugged my shoulders.

"Play."

"You talk to Serena while you're playing, don't you?" she wanted to know. I shook my head.

"What's the matter with you?" she yelled at me. "You never had any trouble talking before. Usually you never stop talking, I don't bring you here every week just to sit there like a stone without opening your mouth. Don't just sit in there, talk to her."

"But Serena says I can just play," I argued. "She says I can do whatever I want to when I'm with her." It was usually hopeless to argue with my mother because she always won, but she was making me really mad this time. As if it wasn't bad enough she felt so ashamed of me that she had to bring me to see Serena once a week, now she wanted me to talk to her, too. I didn't know the name of what was wrong with me, but I knew it had something to do with being too clingy and dependent and whining too much and being too sensitive and the most inconsiderate and self-centered child in the world, and letting other kids pick on me without fighting back, and not knowing how to read yet. And then there was my tunnel dream.

Still, I knew I wasn't really like that boy with his monster head. Anyone who saw him could tell there was something very wrong with him right away. Mine was more on the inside, and if I was very careful, and always paid attention, I might be able to keep it there. That was why I couldn't understand why my mother wanted me to talk to Serena. She had to know that if I talked to her, the part of me that was like the Humpty Dumpty boy would jump out and be revealed. I had figured out that the best policy was to play silently with the toys in Serena's office, and my mother's directions made me feel like I was going to burst in two with the unfairness of it.

As an adult, I asked my mother what possessed her to send me to a psychiatrist at six years old. "It seemed the right thing to do," she said. "In our family. At that time. You never smiled after your sister was born. Not for years." She paused. "Your kindergarten teacher said you had problems. She said you hid in the doll corner. You were afraid of the boys. You know, they were teaching reading in kindergarten then," she said. "You were supposed to know how to read by first grade—and you wouldn't learn."

Our school reading books were full of exciting pictures of children doing things. I spent the long hours when we sat in a circle and took turns sounding out words in the book—so slowly it was impossible to follow the story, which was stupid, anyway—making up stories about the girls in the pictures. By the time it was my turn to read, the teacher always had to call my name twice to get my attention, and I never knew where we were supposed to be. A couple of times I had tried telling her my stories instead of all that boring sounding out, and both times the teacher had smiled at me and said "How nice." She had never acted as if anything was wrong.

I remember the doll corner, too. We had a pink blanket we stretched over the top of two chairs to make a tent. Inside the tent were one brown and two pink Tiny Tears dolls, with eyes that opened and closed, and holes in their mouths and their behinds so when you fed them water with the little bottles, they peed out the other end. You could put them to bed in their cots, under the soft pink light of the blanket tent, and when they were awake you could make up stories about them. There was no fighting or shouting in the doll corner, because no boys were allowed to come in there and bother you, and even the rough girls stayed out. It was by far the best place in the room, and when we were free to play, I saw no reason to go anywhere else.

When I went in to see Serena, my mother stayed outside in the waiting room reading to my little sister Sylvie, who was four, and always wanted to do whatever I did. Sylvie wanted to come in and play with the toys with me, but my mother said she couldn't and that she couldn't tell anyone about Serena, either.

"It's a secret just for us, do you understand?" she asked Sylvie. "If you're a good girl and sit quietly and listen to this book, and if you remember not to talk to anyone about coming here, we'll go out and buy you a new stuffed animal afterwards." My mother knew that I needed no instructions to keep my mouth shut about going to see Serena, but Sylvie was little and had to be told over and over again. It was probably concentration that made my little sister's face pucker up like that, but when I looked at her on the trip home in the car, I thought it was contempt, and was sure she would think of me as her crazy sister for ever and ever, even when we were grown up. It was the ultimate humiliation, and I hit Sylvie until I made her cry whenever we got home from Serena's office.

Serena herself was a tall, gentle, gaunt woman, with green eyes and a cloud of soft silver hair, who bent over or sat on the floor so that she was my height. Because she was the most accommodating adult I had ever met, and the most willing to enter into my games of pretending, it was hard to maintain my resolve to keep quiet. It was not Serena's kindness that finally made me break my vow of silence, however, but a certain cardboard box of paper dolls. All the other toys, including a wonderful doll house and a fair collection of real dolls, were kept out, in big plastic cartons on the floor, but I had found the paper dolls in a secret place, high up in a closet.

"You can look at those," Serena told me, "but you can't play with them. They belong to a big girl who comes in here." There were twelve dolls made out of hard cardboard, each one about about five-inches tall, seven or eight-years old, and distinctly different. After I found them, the only thing I wanted to do when I came to Serena's office was to hold those paper dolls in my hand and let them talk to each other. I hated the big girl who owned them, whom I knew must be another crazy one like the Humpty Dumpty boy, or else why would she come here? I tried not to talk, but it was too much for me. One day I opened my mouth and out popped the very words I had determined not to say. I told Serena I wanted to play with those paper dolls and nothing else. And there it was, my monster badness which had escaped—just as I knew it would. Once it had got out, it would not go back either. I was not content with just asking to play with the dolls once. I whined and begged to play with them. I couldn't stop myself, even though all the time I could hear my mother's angry voice in my head: *All the toys in this office, and you want the one thing you can't have. It's typi-*

cal. The only reason you want those paper dolls is because they belong to someone else. If you got them, you wouldn't want them any more, you'd whine for something else. I knew my mother was right. The proof was in, and now Serena knew I belonged here, just like the Humpty Dumpty boy.

Then it was my birthday, and Serena gave me a long flat box. On the cover there was a picture of all twelve dolls, and when I opened it, there they were. It was a moment of pure joy, holding them, taking them out, and knowing that they were mine—not only to play with in the office, but at home— whenever I wanted to. I had imagined that Serena might tell my mother on me, might stop talking to me, would certainly despise me. I had never foreseen that she would give me the paper dolls, which I had supposed, anyway, to be the only ones of their kind.

As it turned out, I did not stop loving my paper dolls once I had them. Instead, I played with them alone in my room for hours, until I was much too old for dolls. I can still remember Gertrude, a cheap girl who wore make-up and a bra; Audrey, who had red hair and could read perfectly and whom everyone wanted for their best friend; the twins, Elaine and Ann, who dressed alike, did everything together, and were never lonely; and Edith, who had brown, wavy hair and a bad habit of crying in school, who had to go to a psychiatrist, and who all the others despised and called mental and crybaby until Audrey asked her to be her best friend. Every time I spread them out to start the day's story, I felt rich with ill-gotten gains, like the miser in the fairy tale who only had to touch something to make it turn to gold.

When I stopped seeing Serena after we moved to the town the following year, I thought my secret was safe. Then I joined the Brownies and Mrs. Sacrin spoke to me in that special voice, and I knew I had been found out.

Although it has a sad beginning, this story has a happy ending. After two endless years of knots and marching in Brownies, in fourth grade we graduated to Girl Scouts—and to a leader named Mrs. Thompson who told us she worked with Negro Brownies and Girls Scouts in a settlement house in Millwood. I had heard about Millwood before. It was a poor, slummy part of the city where Negroes had to live because people were prejudiced against them, just like the Nazis had been prejudiced against the Jews. Mrs. Thompson thought marching and knots were silly and asked us what we wanted to do instead. Inspired, I suggested that we put on a play for the Negro kids. As I could read and write very well by that time, I volunteered to write it myself. I went home that night, got out my *Grimms' Fairy Tales,* and in a businesslike way, turned the story of Rumpelstiltskin into a play in three acts of rhyming verse.

I worked especially hard, and with real satisfaction, on the part of the princess, for which I had Debby Hahn in mind. I didn't anticipate any argument about this casting because everyone knew princesses had to have long blonde hair and blue eyes, but to be on the safe side, I added stage directions in which I specified these characteristics. Debby Hahn was a new girl in our school whom I didn't know that well because she was in the second to top class and I was in the top one, but, like everyone else in the fourth grade, I had heard the shocking news—Debby Hahn left school early every Friday afternoon to go to a psychiatrist. This was no mere rumor: Debby had told the kids in her class herself. She had just moved to our town from California, which I thought must account for this terrible mistake on her part, and also for the way she dressed—in light blue, yellow, or pink dresses as flouncy and pretty as a sugar Easter egg. These things, along with the damning habits of crying in school and telling on other kids, were enough to make her a pariah whom no one but me talked to, except to scream *mental cooties, mental cooties* at her.

Every time someone made fun of her, Debby Hahn cried. Sometimes she even cried for no reason at all that anyone could see. She had very light, almost milky blue eyes, usually pink from crying, skin that was a transparent blue-white color instead of pink like everybody else's, and hair that was not goldy blonde like the horse girls' hair, but a yellowish white like the overcooked yoke of a hard-boiled egg, so long and thick she could sit on it when she wore it loose. Most of the time, though, she wore it in a tight ponytail, which made the transparent skin at her temples taut, an effect I especially admired. Sidney, who had tried to talk to her once or twice, thought she was stupid and pathetic, but I thought she was beautiful. I told Sidney, who only shrugged instead of acting jealous like she was supposed to, that I was going to be Debby Hahn's friend no matter what. At night I imagined rescuing her from the others and holding her in my arms as she wept. *You know, Rachel, I don't need my psychiatrist, now that I have you.*

Before Girl Scouts offered me the perfect opportunity, I had already done everything I knew how to make friends with Debby Hahn. I had tried to get the others to leave her alone at recess, but they only called me mental too, while she went inside to tell the teacher on them. Another time I approached her when she was crying for no apparent reason and asked her what was wrong, but she only sniffed and gulped and turned her back on me. I had even tried inviting her home with me after school, something that you weren't supposed to do with kids from a lower group unless they lived next door to you or your parents were friends or something, but Debby told me that going to other people's houses made her nervous, and refused. I myself was afraid to stay overnight at anyone's house, a shameful fact I tried my best to conceal from everyone. Something about the way Debby didn't seem to realize that there was anything wrong with being mental fascinated and amazed me, and I would not give up my quest.

When she showed up in Girl Scouts, looking pale and pretty in the olive green uniform which had succeeded the brown one, and which made all the rest of us look yellowish, I knew this was my chance. Debby Hahn was a born princess, and she would not, could not, refuse the part. What fourth-grade girl could? I was convinced that even Sidney, who despised such things and was not in Girl Scouts anyway, would have thought twice before letting such an opportunity go. I had even allowed myself some wistful thoughts about blonde wigs, but really I knew better than to aspire to princesshood myself. Even with a blonde wig, I was just not the type. Instead, as the author and, with Mrs. Thompson, the codirector of the play, I modestly gave myself the small but juicy part of a witch, a role that allowed me to stand with my broomstick on the sidelines, stirring my brew and coaching Debby Hahn on her lines.

After months of rehearsals, we performed the play one afternoon in Mrs. Thompson's settlement house, on a stage with a red velvety curtain that really pulled, for an appreciative audience of three troops of small brown-skinned Brownies. They screamed in terror when Rumpelstiltskin stamped his feet and called down the curse, and hugged each other and shivered when the witch came on.

Even after my gift of the princess's part, Debby Hahn had not wanted to be my friend, but by that time I didn't really care. During the rehearsals I'd found out she was stupid, just like Sidney had said. I'd had to rewrite the princess's part twice: once so that she had only a few lines to say, and again so that she just came on in the second act, giving her plenty of time to get over her nervousness. Still, when mental Debby Hahn—with her yellow hair loose, her jeweled crown shining, and the special royal blue princess dress her mother had sewn for her—made her first appearance, and all the Brownies in the audience let out a collective moan, *Ooo. . .*, I felt a little the way I did when Serena had first given me the paper dolls and I spread them all out on my lap. It eased something in my heart.

AWARDS

BY THE THIRD GRADE WE ALL KNEW, DESPITE
THE EVIDENCE OF OUR OWN SENSES, THAT BOYS WERE
smarter than girls. Science had proven it. The only reason all
the smartest kids in our class were girls was that girls matured
earlier. By the seventh and eighth grades, the grownups assured
us, Elizabeth Carlson and Susan Doralski would already have
passed their prime and would have to yield up their places to
some hitherto undistinguished boy, like Chester Laughton or
Charlie Nails, who might even go straight on to be President,
while Elizabeth and Susan could only hope to wait at home for
them, ironing their shirts and packing their kids' lunchboxes
with nutritional snacks.

Our head start on maturity, although nothing to write
home about in the long run, was at least supposed to provide
us girls with good penmanship, a skill which boys were supposed to lack. The monthly Penmanship Award was generally

acknowledged to be a contest for the girls. It was the only contest, except for sports, that involved collective rather than individual achievement. It was also the only one in which the high and low classes competed against each other. The way it worked was that on a certain day of the month, every child in every class was asked to copy out the same passage—something about a lazy but fast-jumping brown fox—in our very best cursive, using special ball-point pens and white paper. All these passages were collected and sent away to the Penmanship Inspector, an important man who lived somewhere else. I pictured him as sitting in the top room of a castle like the Wizard's in the Emerald City, served by pages who, bending down on one knee, offered him silver trays full of penmanship.

After a few weeks the Penmanship Inspector sent down his verdict, which the teachers announced solemnly in a special grade-wide ceremony involving the exchange of the scrolls which held the penmanship seals. These embossed, heraldic seals were awarded to the room as a whole, and were kept on the class bulletin board all month long. Like the ribbons the horse girls won for riding and scotchtaped to the insides of their lockers, the seals came in five shiny colors: gold, silver, blue, red, and shameful green. Each large scroll contained one of the seals and an inscription, in the very finest cursive, proclaiming it an award for *excellent, very good, good, average,* or *poor* work in Penmanship.

As in all group efforts, extremes counted too much. Susan Doralski, an earnest, strangely wooden girl who lived on my street, who often consulted me as we waited for the morning bus about how to act in various situations, or about what a certain kid had really meant by what she said, had an uncanny ability to produce writing just like the writing on the scroll. Susan was our greatest asset, with Mandy Sacrin, the Brownie leader's goody-goody daughter who, Sidney and I were convinced, spent hours practicing her perfectly round, perfectly even handwriting, not far behind. But our top third-grade class never got the gold seal all year, and I was sure it was all because of me. No matter how much I tried, my writing came out wobbly, different shapes and sizes, refusing to stay inside the lines. Such aberrant handwriting would have been O.K. for a boy—it might even be a sign of budding genius. But for a girl it was something of a disgrace. As the only girl with bad handwriting, I was convinced that even my very best effort always kept our class at red, or blue at best.

Our third-grade teacher, Mrs. Blanchard, tried to use the penmanship competition to bring our class down a peg or two, as the grownups used to say.

"Shame on you! You let 3B beat you again," she reproached us every month, but no one but Susan Doralski took her very seriously. The kids in my class knew that no competition that 3B could win really counted. Also, while decent handwriting was important for girls, excessively good handwriting was a somewhat dubious quality for anyone. For a boy, it meant being a sissy. For a girl, it meant maturity, a state we weren't sure we wanted that much. Not only did girls get it faster than boys and end up dumber in the end, but everyone knew that the girls in the low groups matured faster than we did and would probably all be wearing bras by fifth grade. Although I could tell Mrs. Blanchard was upset by my classmates' monthly accusations and the fingers which pointed at me when we failed once again to win the gold seal, I bore the ritual stoically, as an annoyance rather than a major humiliation. All this changed at the end-of-the-year awards ceremony.

The real awards for our grade had already been given out, and it was Penmanship's turn. Mrs. Blanchard presented Susan Doralski with the first prize, a book on handwriting around the world, and Mandy Sacrin with an honorable mention, a rather superior ball-point pen. We all clapped, pleased with the justice of it. Then she paused impressively and announced a special, new award for "The most improvement in Penmanship—and for all around improvement—to Rachel!" Dazed, I advanced to the front of the room, where, with a special flourish and a warm smile, Mrs. Blanchard presented me with the scroll containing the same gold seal which my bad handwriting had kept our room from ever winning. I remember the half-hearted, embarrassed clapping, the slimy feel of that glossy piece of paper, and how, returning to my seat, I looked away from Sidney's pitying face.

The most improvement. Those words stuck in my throat like a stone. I knew what they meant. It was a consolation prize for the crazy person—the one who had something wrong with her and had been sent to Serena. It was a fake award invented especially for the one with the very worst penmanship of all, the one who could never win a real award, to fool her and make her feel better. Looking back on it I imagine Mrs. Blanchard must have felt pleased with her idea for the new award—a way to make up, at one stroke, for my monthly teasing and raise my status with my peers.

Grownups must have thought we were stupid, really, because they were always trying things like that, praising kids who hadn't done anything special and inventing fake awards for kids who didn't deserve them. Mrs. Blanchard was a nice teacher, with red hair and soft pink-and-white freckled arms, who had never spoken to me with anything sticky in her voice, or anything different than the way she spoke to all of us, until she gave me that award. I dreaded bringing the gold seal home to show my mother, who, I knew, would understand what it really was.

Quite different was the award I got for my book report from the town library earlier that same year. My mother tells me that soon after we moved to the town, when I was in the second grade, she became fed up with the school's ineffectual efforts and taught me to read herself. It must have been a fairly painless process because I remember nothing about it. In my own memory, being able to read was a gift that descended on me suddenly like manna from heaven, at the same time as I learned to ride my bike.

After that I could ride to school on my own in the morning, with Dusty running panting behind me. She lay patiently waiting for me in the shade next to my bike all day, and then when school was over, followed after Sidney and me as we biked to the solid red brick town library. Much later I encountered the lines *luxe, calme, et volupté,* and recognized the feeling I got every time I opened the library door and contemplated the rows and rows of books I hadn't yet read, then curled up with four or five of them in the big green leather window seat. Sidney and I were both reading all the biographies of famous people, a set of grown-up looking thick orange books which took up a whole shelf in the library. Amelia Earhart and Abe Lincoln were the best, we agreed. The people in books, who before I learned to read were a gift my mother conferred on me every night when she read to me, were suddenly there, waiting for me whenever I wanted them—after I got home from school, on weekends, or at night when I was supposed to be asleep, under the covers with a flashlight. I didn't need my mother any more to spend time with Jo March or *Anne of Green Gables* or Sarah Crewe or Mary Lennox of *The Secret Garden*—I had a life of my own.

The librarians were Mrs. Felix, an old, strict-looking lady with a bony face, a limp, and a permanently hoarse voice, and Mrs. Bride, who was younger, plump, and more friendly. They both talked like the horse girls' mothers, but I could tell they liked me and took me seriously. When Mrs. Bride put her finger to her chin, gazed at me, and thought as hard as she could about which book to recommend to me next, I could tell she was seeing an especially smart, ordinary girl, not one with something wrong with her. Sometimes even Mrs. Felix, who everyone was scared of, and who rarely spoke to children except to rasp at them to be quiet or leave, would emerge from her special office at the top of the stairs and beckon me with a crooked arthritic finger to come up to her so she could recommend a book. The librarians, especially Mrs. Bride, were my friends, but when I wanted to take out books from the grown-up part of the library, they exchanged glances, hesitated, and said they would have to ask my mother. It was because grown-up books had sex in them, my mother explained. Lots of grown-ups thought children should be ignorant about sex, but that was a superstition, like believing in God. Sigmund Freud had discovered that children knew all about sex anyway, and so she had a talk with the librarians and I was allowed to take out any book in the whole library.

When I learned to read, I worried that my mother might be mad at me for deserting her and that she would stop reading with me, but she didn't. We still read together every night, only now we took turns reading, and sometimes we read poems and books in French. She told me about grown-up books that had children in them, mostly orphans like Jane Eyre, who had to make their own way in the world without a friend. I loved books like that because after I stopped reading them I could go on with them in my head, with myself as the orphan's friend and rescuer. Other books she told me about were ones she had read as a child—*Buddenbrooks* and *The Three Musketeers*—and the books she had read to learn English—*The Great Gatsby, The Grapes of Wrath,* and *The Wasteland.* The last and best of these was by a writer called Jo Sinclair, who was really a woman, only she'd had to pretend to be a man when she wrote the book because it was hard for women to be writers in those days. It was about a man who went to see a psychiatrist because he had a bad childhood and hated himself, and he told the psychiatrist about all the different Passovers he had ever had, and in the end he got cured and wasn't embarrassed to be Jewish any more and changed his name from Jack back to Jake and helped his parents and took his nephews to a baseball game so they wouldn't turn out bad the way he had. After that his sister Debby, who was my favorite character, didn't have to be the man of the family any more. Debby had light blonde very short hair, only wore pants, and never went out with men, just with her best friend who was a Negro girl. She took care of the whole family, and it was Jake's fault she had turned out like that. I especially liked to think about Debby at night. When the library announced its book report contest, however, I decided to pick not *The Wasteland* or any of the other fat books from the grown-up section, but my favorite book of all, *Baby Island.*

Baby Island was the story of two girls, nine and eleven, who were shipwrecked on a desert island with no grownups, but a whole shipload of babies whom they took care of by themselves. I remember copying the report several times, bad penmanship and all, full of that slightly tremulous but satisfying feeling I still get after having written something that comes from my deepest self. I won the Grand Prize, a silver cup, for that report, and knew that I deserved it.

It was easy to tell the fake awards from the real. Another fake one, established when I was in junior high school, was the Good Citizenship Award, something the grownups invented for the kids who would never win the academic awards: those in the middle and low groups, though never the very lowest; the many nice girls and fewer nice boys who always tried hard and never got in trouble; the boys who, in high school, coached the teams but never played on them; and the girls who joined Future Homemakers of America and decorated the gym for the dances they never attended. Sidney and I used to dread these citizenship awards. We sat during the assemblies devoted to them avoiding each other's eyes and blushing. We never questioned the fact that the world and everyone in it was ordered from best to worst, but it seemed like needless cruelty on the part of the grownups to invent fake awards which fooled nobody and only rubbed it in.

The last fake award, given in eighth grade, when we had all heard about the Civil Rights Movement, was the D.A.R. Award. Sidney had told me all about the D.A.R. Her mother was always getting calls from ladies who wanted her to join it, since she had come over on the Mayflower, but she refused because she said it was vulgar. Polly's and Sal's and the horse girls' mothers were invited to be in it too, but they all said no.

The D.A.R. meant Daughters of the American Revolution, and it stood for everything bad: the policy the next town over from ours had of not letting Jews buy a house there; the South —and lynchings and segregated water fountains and how Negroes couldn't vote there or buy a cup of coffee at a lunch counter; the John Birch Society; and burning books. Only vulgar people like Mandy Sacrin's mother, who was Catholic and hadn't really come over on the Mayflower with Sidney's mother anyway, but only liked to pretend she had, were in it.

Our town had no Black families during all the years I lived in it, and before we came, no Jews either. New people who wanted to move in had to be able to afford an acre and a half of land along with their house. I was never invited to the country club dances Sidney and Sal and the horse girls were asked to, and almost all the Catholic kids were stuck forever in the lowest groups and would not be able to go on to college. Sidney and I didn't think about any of these things, but we did make a mental list of all the eighth-grade girls who had gotten the D.A.R. Award in previous years. There had been Melanie King, who was legally blind; Ann Robinson, who'd had polio and walked with a brace; and Trixie Ushida, who was almost a horse girl, and very popular, but who was Chinese or Japanese —we weren't sure which. We figured that there hadn't been any foreign kids in the town at first, so they'd had to give it to kids with something wrong with them, but obviously the award was meant to trick us into believing the D.A.R. wasn't prejudiced after all.

Sidney was clearly not at risk for this year's prize, we reasoned, but I, as the only Jewish girl, was a prime candidate. We spent hours composing a speech of rejection, just in case, and Sidney coached me on it as I sat on the horse-tying posts in front of her house where we used to play Electric Chair.

As it worked out, I didn't get to make our speech. They gave the D.A.R. Award to Beryl Wong, the only Chinese girl in our grade, who went up to the stage to accept it with her head down, as though she might burst into tears. We turned away and never spoke of it again.

EENY MEENY MINY MO

EENY MEENY MINY MO, WE COUNTED. *CATCH THE TIGGER BY THE TOE.* I HAD ALWAYS SAID IT THAT way but I'd heard other, bad kids say it the other way. It was about the worst word you could say, much worse than swears like *fuck* or *shit,* which didn't harm anyone, my mother said, though they weren't very nice. It was like calling a Jew a kike, and if any Negro heard someone say it, they would be very hurt. It was not likely that any Negro would hear the word *nigger* at that time and in that town because no Negroes lived there.

There were no Black students in my class until high school, but there was always Beryl Wong, whose father was a professor at the same college as Kai St. Clair's. My father said he was a famous scientist, very well-known in his field, and the Wongs had a tennis court and a fish pond with giant goldfish and turtles right inside their house, so they had to be rich, but none of that counted, not in the same way. Beryl Wong was the only person I knew whose grandmother lived with them, and she couldn't speak English. Beryl's mother could speak English, but with a Chinese accent. When my mother talked on the dictaphone, which was the only time I could hear her accent, her words came out louder and harsher, with every sound clear and distinct, but Beryl's mother talked in such a soft whispery voice that you could hardly hear her, and she seemed to swallow half the sounds in the words. Mrs. Wong was a pretty, willowy woman who was always beautifully dressed in dresses made out of special soft wool with matching silky scarves, and her glossy black hair was always gently waved, as though she'd just had it done. She smiled nervously at the school's open houses, looking at the floor instead of the teachers' faces, and said thank you too often, in her soft whispery voice.

Although we were polite to each other, Beryl and I were not friends. We never invited each other over or talked in school. Beryl only invited over Kai or Biscuit or other horse girls, who I didn't think were really her friends at all, though they let her sit with them in the lunchroom and be in their clubs. Sometimes she invited Sal Winter, whom I occasionally invited over too, and it was Sal who told me about the tennis court and the fish pond.

The first and only time I went to Beryl Wong's house was for a birthday party in the fourth grade, the year when all the girls whose mothers would let them had giant birthday parties to which they invited all the girls in the class. My mother had sewn puppets for each of the thirteen girls at my party: clowns with bells and round, grinning mouths, red devils with pointed ears and tails, princesses with crowns and long flowing hair, and Davy Crocketts with real fur hats. Everyone had to agree that nothing could match that, but the prizes at Beryl's party were next best. They were little Chinese pincushion dolls that opened in the middle to reveal secret boxes, smooth wooden puzzles that wouldn't get back together once you took them apart, purses that lay flat until you opened them out into one long rectangle, and fragile fans that swung open to reveal pictures of butterflies and pink flowers. At my party we'd had hot dogs, potato

chips, birthday cake, and square three-colored ice cream—
exactly the food you were supposed to have at birthday
parties—but at Beryl's party there was fried chicken and potato
salad, and for desert, along with the birthday cake, amazing
strawberry sherbet in the shape of a swan, and a fortune cookie
for everyone. Beryl's grandmother had been hidden somewhere
for the whole party, but she came out, by mistake, right at the
end. Beryl turned on her, and scolded her in Chinese in a loud,
quick voice quite different from her usual one, and her grandmother went away again. I remember her limping on tiny feet,
but surely she was too young for bound feet? It must have been
the long, narrow skirt she wore that made her walk that way.

The Wong's house was two houses really, connected by a
roofed courtyard that held the famous fish pond. Beryl's father
had designed them both and built one for his family and one
for his brother's family to live in. The two twin houses stood
on several acres on a hill in the most expensive of the new
developments—two beautiful, delicate companion houses built
of redwood, quite different from anything else in the town.

Beryl herself was a slightly chunky, pretty girl whose teeth
stuck out until she got her braces off, unlike mine, which, as
far as I could see, stuck out just as much as they did before. Even
without her braces, she almost never smiled all the way. She
wore her straight black hair curled under and sometimes held
back with a barrette, just like all the top girls' hair, and the way
mine refused to go, no matter how tightly I rolled it in curlers
every night. Beryl bought her clothes at The Country Store the
way the horse girls did, and wore Fair Isle sweaters and penny
loafers like them, but it was not, could never be, the same. Her
clothes were too new looking, and they always matched, with
the yoke of the sweater picking up the color of the skirt. They
were always perfectly clean and carefully ironed. Even her
loafers, which were supposed to be scuffed, looked as though
she polished them every morning.

Beryl Wong got on my nerves in school because she
seemed to lack any backbone. If a teacher asked her what she
thought, she would shrug and look down at her desk in an

agony of shyness. The only time she ever raised her hand was to nod her head in agreement with something one of the horse girls had said. You couldn't rely on her to stand behind you in plans against the grownups, either, like the time Sidney and I arranged for everyone in the class to stop paying attention to our horrible French teacher, Mr. Trojanian. When you asked Beryl if you could count on her for something like that, she would shrug and nod, but when the time came she would look around to find out what the popular kids were doing before she joined in.

All these things were minor compared to the truly terrible thing about Beryl Wong, which everyone knew but tried not to say out loud: that she habitually cheated on tests. How she cheated was so embarrassing and weird that all of us, even the teachers, tried to pretend it wasn't happening. Because she was never exactly caught, Beryl was also never humiliated in public, the way Mr. Douglass, the science teacher, humiliated Bridget Corcoran, a new Catholic kid who moved to town in seventh grade and got placed in the top class by mistake. Bridget Corcoran's mother worked as the receptionist for the doctor most of us went to, and nobody had ever heard of her having a father. She teased her reddish blonde hair on top and wore very bright pink lipstick. When Mr. Douglass caught her copying off Susan Doralski's test paper, he made her stand up in front of the room and told her she was despicable, and maybe that was the way they acted where she came from, but it wasn't the kind of behavior we put up with in our school, until she started to sob in front of the whole class, and someone whispered, "Look at her eye make-up run!" We all felt a little sorry for Bridget, but I don't remember blaming Mr. Douglass too much. It seemed inevitable, somehow. Bridget Corcoran was switched out of our class soon after that, and her family moved a few years later.

Beryl Wong's cheating was a different story. If you sat near her during a test or a quiz, you could sometimes see her needing to do it, reasoning with herself, clenching her hands together and digging her nails into the flesh of them, then suddenly giving up and sneaking a look at the paper next to hers. When the need was on her, Beryl cheated from whoever happened to be sitting nearby, even from Brian Moody or Charlie Nichols, bad top boys who never did any work and were sure not to have the right answers. If Beryl really needed to cheat, Sidney and I used to wonder, why didn't she cheat from Susan Doralski, who had never been known to get anything but 100 on multiple-choice tests, or from Elizabeth Carlson or Davy Cohen? In fact, as we all knew, Beryl didn't need to cheat. She was one of the smartest kids in our top class who usually got *B+* on everything, though her report cards always said she could do *A* work if she only had more confidence. Beryl's worst subject was French because she refused to speak it out loud, although she never got anything wrong on grammar tests.

One time, Beryl started to cheat off Charlie Nichols' science quiz, and Mandy Sacrin poked Caro Warner and pointed, and then all of a sudden everyone, even Mr. Douglass, was staring at Beryl, who was leaning over and copying answers as fast as she could. It was so obvious that ignoring it would have been even more embarrassing than saying something about it, but Mr. Douglass didn't make Beryl stand up in front of the class like he had Bridget. He just went over to her desk and quietly asked her to stay after school to talk to him.

Do I really remember hearing what Mr. Douglass said to Beryl Wong behind closed doors that day? Did Sidney and I press our ears up against the door, listening, or am I making it up? I know we used to discuss Beryl's cheating—along with other aberrations like Elizabeth Carlson's fits and Susan Doralski's strange innocence—with some fascination, concluding that it was a disease, like kleptomania, but it is hard to imagine us taking the risk of stationing ourselves by the door. And I wonder why all the cheating scenes I remember are set in Mr. Douglass's cold science room, with metal desks so high that you had to sit at them with special metal stools, tubby, important black microscopes that came up from inside the desks, steel sinks and bunson burners for experiments, and the dank smell of the paraldehyde used for dissecting frogs. What I may remember Mr. Douglass saying is *Beryl, why did you do it? You don't need to cheat, your answers were right. Charlie Nichols' were wrong, you must have known that. Why?* But that might have been only what I would have said in his place. And I think she sat mute, tears rolling down her cheeks, not saying anything back, though I certainly could not have seen this. She was a silent girl, Beryl Wong. It was agony for her to speak up. The top kids were always electing her to be secretary of something, Student Council or Band or Select Chorus or Homeroom, because it looked good to have a Chinese girl as an officer, and she was smart, and very obedient, always inviting them to her beautiful house, always sniffing around those top kids. As secretary, Beryl turned in perfect notes in her neat, rounded handwriting and didn't interrupt their meetings by saying one word.

BUMBLEBEES AND DINING ROOM SETS

THE FIRST NONWHITE PERSON I KNEW BE-
SIDES BERYL WONG WAS A GIRL AT THE SUMMER DAY CAMP
I went to when I was seven, the summer after second grade. A
camp for very young children held on the grounds of the town's
art museum, it was a blessed interval of peace after the tense
and exciting atmosphere of school with its competition for
friends and success. Every day we were given blank sheets of
paper, clay, sketch pads, scraps, and materials to build with, and
encouraged to have fun. We made our art in big white canvas
tents on the museum grounds and played in the surrounding
gardens, where the grass was as soft as velvet and there were
huge trees with private shady caves inside the branches, with
floors of papery dead leaves. I remember some kind of Grecian
or Roman theme: At the end of the summer we all wore white
muslin togas tied with gold cords and there was an enormous
papier-mâché Trojan horse, broken open one day in an excit-

ing ceremony, with people coming out.

The Black girl must have been younger than me, maybe six or even five to my seven, because my memory of her is of a much smaller, exquisite girl with whom I played house in the tree caves, in a decorous and calm way, with none of the inventiveness or fierce energy that play with Sidney required. Unless it was called baby-sitting, adults usually frowned on older children playing with younger ones; they called you immature and implied that children your own age were too much for you if you ever tried it. I had always respected this prohibition, but that summer the adults must have lifted it for the two of us. They smiled at us benignly, pleased I suppose, at the picture we made. Except for my sister Sylvie, whom I bullied unmercifully, I was not used to playing with younger children, and playing with the little girl, I experienced, perhaps for the first time, that strong surge of protectiveness which flooded my body with warmth, and which I would later associate with being in love: *I'll take care of you. I won't let anything bad happen to you.*

I remember her color, which was a dark, rich chocolate, and that she had long hair, pulled tightly into a ponytail of a dense, very soft consistency, like cotton candy, except for a few curling tendrils around her face. I don't think I knew that she was something called a Negro, but I noticed the way things looked on her: her bright one-piece playsuits with colorful patterns of butterflies or flowers, the white smock she wore for painting, made, like all of ours, out of one of her daddy's white shirts, and the toga. I was very skinny at that age, but quite tall, and my skin got covered with freckles in the summer. I felt disappointed with the way I looked in my toga, with my long whitish, freckled legs coming out of the bottom of the whitish freckled material. I much preferred the look of her in it, the small rounded compactness of her, and the contrast of her glowing brown skin with the pale gold-flecked material. Now, as I think of her, I suddenly can see her sandals, which were tiny, white, and ornamented with the most beautiful fake jewels, green and ruby. My memories of her are decorative, and she seemed to me altogether a most beautifully ornamented girlchild, quite different from the girls at school, whose summer wear was blue-jean shorts, white T-shirts, and old sneakers. For summer shoes I wore red boxy snub-nosed sandals that looked as if they'd had bits cut out with cookie cutters, and I envied those jeweled sandals with all my heart.

One day the girl, whose name I cannot remember, only that it, too, was unusual and decorative—something like Philomena or Laetitia or Felicia—got stung by a bumblebee. It hovered over her with its gold-and-black body, like the body of those fuzzy bear caterpillars we used to carry tenderly and put in a jar where we would sometimes find them, dried up, days later. I think she was scared of it and I told her not to be, it was just a bee, and then she got stung and cried, bitterly and inconsolably. I stood by stricken—full of guilt at having failed to protect her, a desperate desire to comfort her, and a feeling of helplessness when I could not.

The sting must have happened late in the day because soon after, her father came to pick her up—a handsome man, the originator of her white smock—and she hurled herself into his arms, crying again for his benefit. He lifted her up high in the air and turned to all of us with a kind of fury, demanding to know what had happened to his little girl. The counselors hastened to explain that no one had hurt her, no one had abused her, it had been only a bee, a part of nature, unavoidable, but she'd become quite upset, had had quite a reaction to it. I hovered, watching, near tears myself, until some adult saw me and reassured me: Felicia would be alright, it was just a bee sting, I shouldn't worry.

"Those two are so cute," I heard one of them say. "Look how worried she is about her friend!" I was glad they thought that. It was better than if they knew the truth: that when I saw that the girl had never once looked to me for comfort, only to the counselors and then her father, it was like falling off my bike hard, in that first moment when I'd wonder if I was dead or alive. I had felt just as big and as loving to Felicia as any grownup, but now I realized that I was nobody to her, really, just another little kid. Was I also sad because of the way in which that tall, commanding father had picked her up, when my own father would have been embarrassed by my tears, muttered to me not to be a crybaby, it was just a bee, and on the way home warned me not to tell my mother of my disgrace?

I don't remember being told that the little girl was a Negro, but someone must have said it because I defined the term accordingly. Years later, when I was ten and in fifth grade, our whole grade, along with all the fifth graders from the nearby airforce base, went to a wilderness center in New Hampshire for three days. There was a girl in the bunk below me whom I talked to, and later I commented to Sidney that I had liked that Chinese girl. She told me with great contempt that that girl was a Negro, I sure was stupid, didn't I even know what a Negro was? No, I insisted, sure that I was right for once, the girl was Chinese. After all, she was a golden yellow color, almost the same as Beryl Wong's, and her hair stuck out in a straight thick mass like Beryl's. I knew that Negro girls were a deep chocolate color, with a mass of soft hair, and I refused to yield my point, until, infuriated, Sidney appealed to someone else.

"You won't believe this! Rachel thought that Negro girl in the bottom bunk was Chinese!" Whoever it was laughed, and I was ashamed and confused, and swore to myself that I would keep my mouth shut and never identify anyone as anything again, until someone else had said it first.

Why do I remember the girl at day camp as my first sight of a Black person, my one reference for the second girl? Is it because, for very young children, only other children are really people and grownups belong to a foreign species of their own? In the city, when I was very young, before we moved to the town, there was Norma, who baby-sat for me on the days my mother went to work, before my sister was born as well as after, though I don't remember Sylvie there, only Norma and me, Norma talking and me listening. Maybe my sister was too small to listen or to be talked to, a silent presence wheeled along in a baby carriage, or maybe I was so infuriated at her entry into the family that I blocked her out, even in memory.

Norma was terribly tall, though I don't know if she was really tall for a grownup or not. I think she was dark, more the color of the little girl at camp than Beryl Wong, but while the little girl was a vibrant, moist earth color, Norma was a dusty greyish brown. I think she must have been weary and preoccupied, because she walked too fast, pulling me along by the wrist the way my mother never did. She took me with her on the subway, jerking me over the gap between the platform and the train with her strong arm, and telling me, every time, that lots of little girls had fallen into that hole and been run over by the train and killed dead, so I better watch out.

Norma talked to me about her son, who was bad and always in trouble, and about bedroom sets, living room sets, and dining room sets, and her perpetual struggle to obtain them. She kept putting down a down payment, but then, every single time, her son would get in trouble and the store would take it back, and there she was, right back where she started from. Once there was even a fire, and it burned part of a bedroom set. Fires seemed to happen a lot. One time she was in the the subway and smelled smoke and no one would believe her, they never did, and they wouldn't stop the train until the tunnel had filled up with smoke and everyone had almost been killed, and then when she got home another piece of her bedroom set had gone, just like that, because no one believed her, even though she had been right all along.

Norma took me home with her a few times, where I met her son—a big boy/man with a long head and no hair, who gave me an unfriendly look which I didn't take personally, as I had heard from Norma all about how bad he was. I remember closely packed, solid brown furniture with feet like deers' hooves, and my sense that these pieces of furniture might come alive at any moment and walk away.

Usually Norma took me to the park where I could find my friend Foxy, who lived inside one of the statues of a soldier, and would come out if I ran around the statue three times and said the magic words. I was relieved that Norma never interfered with this, or wanted to know the magic words or anything else about Foxy, the way my mother did when she came to the park with me. My mother thought it would be nice if she could meet Foxy herself and asked me if it was a boy or a girl, which I couldn't answer. It was neither. It was something else, not a person at all, and anyway, Foxy wasn't something to talk about out loud, it was secret. My mother also wanted me to tell her that I knew Foxy was just pretend, a betrayal which would certainly make it decide never to come again if it heard, and which I refused to do. Although I wouldn't have admitted it, it was sometimes more relaxing going to the park with Norma, who didn't ask me for anything, only talked to me about herself and was glad when I disappeared for a while to see Foxy, leaving her to sit on the green blistered bench and talk to the other ladies.

Did I really fail to classify Norma with the Black girl at camp only because she belonged to the grownups and Felicia to the children? I think I also must have had a sense that the little girl, with her jeweled sandals, her handsome father, and her assumption that she would be looked after, belonged to the world of privilege and of parents who paid attention to you, just as I did, and as Norma and her son clearly did not. There is a kind of knowing without words, and even at four years old, I felt that Norma was not a grownup in the same way my mother was. Maybe it was because she talked to me about her troubles— about the disappearing living room sets and money and her son and fires on the subway—as if I were a grownup myself, instead of focusing her attention on me in the way my parents and teachers did. I didn't know Norma was a Negro, but I did know she was different, that her life was bad and unpredictable, that fires and police and furniture being taken away could happen to her, that she had to be careful and watch out, almost as if she were a child like me who could get tricked: sucked down into the subway hole, trapped in a tunnel for crazy people, or caught and stuck in an oven—not a real grownup, like my teachers or my mother, who knew everything, and to whom nothing bad could ever happen.

THE NAZIS AND THE COOTIES

ONLY SOME OF US WERE MEANT TO BE ALIVE IN THE WORLD. MY FRIENDS SIDNEY AND MERRILL, AND my rival Sal Winter, were meant to be alive, but not me or my sister or brother or one half of Danny Cramer whose father was ordinary but whose mother limped and talked with an accent.

"If the Nazis had caught Mrs. Cramer," I asked my mother when I was seven or eight, "what would have happened to Danny?"

"Think it out for yourself, Schnuckie," my mother said. "Would there even be a Danny?" If the Nazis had caught Mrs. Cramer, I thought it out, Mr. Cramer would have had to marry someone else, someone who wasn't Jewish. There would be a Danny, but he would have come out tall and brave with a deep voice like Bill Adams, not small and squeaky-voiced and always trying to make people like him by being a clown. But both my parents were Jewish, and if Hitler had caught them the way he was supposed to, I would not exist at all. They would have been gassed in ovens when they were teenagers, and made into glue or lampshades or piled on enormous stacks of bodies to rot, and I would be a blank, a nothing at all.

One friend of my parents, Anya Schwartz, walked with a limp like Mrs. Cramer, and it was because the Nazis had run her over. In my picture of how it had been, she was walking down a dusty dirt road, tired out from working all day with no food, and they came up behind her in a tank, three blond, blue-eyed young men sitting together in the front seat, and they ran her over just for the fun of it. I thought maybe after they ran her over they had put her in one of those hospitals I had read about where they did experiments on women, and that was why she and her husband Morey didn't have any children, just three little dogs, Karli and Rosa and Leon. When we went to their house I played with the little dogs and tried not to look at the greyish blue number tattooed on the back of Anya's hand. My mother said some people had them removed after, but other people didn't—they wanted the world to remember.

I thought the Germans must be the worst of anybody, but my mother said they weren't. "So it happened to be the Germans," she said. "It could have been anyone. People are sheep, they move in a herd, a pack, they go along with anything if others are doing it, I told you, they were just following orders. You think the French helped us once the Nazis came? You think the Americans and the English were so eager to save the Jews? Nobody wanted them messing up their nice country."

"Then how did you escape?" I asked her. "How did you come here if nobody wanted the Jews? My mother shrugged. "We were lucky" she said. "There was money. We had connections. My mother was smart, she could see what was coming."

If my grandmother had escaped by being smart, I thought maybe it was only the stupid people who had stayed behind and got caught, but my mother said no, it could have happened to anyone. "Don't let anyone try to tell you the Jews died because they didn't try to run or because they didn't fight back," she said.

"They died whether they fought back or not. It was an accident, just an accident who got saved."

"Tell me about when you escaped from the camp?" I asked my father. "I told you already about it lots of times," he said. "It was in France. I hit a guard on his head, *cnack!,* and we all run. For weeks I ate only raw potatoes from the fields."

"But why didn't you ask someone for some food? A French person?" "Ask? I told you already, if the French had seen me they would have right away turned me in. I told you the story before. You know I don't like to talk about this. Why do you keep asking me?"

"But in school they said the French were against the Germans," I said, and he shrugged, just like my mother had. "French, Germans—who cared about the Jews? Now we talk about something else."

I'd liked it better when it was just the Germans who were the bad ones. I knew they had a wall in the middle of their country now, the Berlin Wall, which would stop them from getting together and doing it again. When President Kennedy got elected, Robert Frost read a poem that went, *Something there is that doesn't like a wall,* but it didn't mean he was for the Nazis. He was for peace. He was an old man and couldn't see to read his poem, but at the end, though, he recited it by heart because he was a great writer, like I was going to be when I grew up.

If the Germans were not the bad ones, it could be anyone, anyone at all. After we saw the concentration camp movie at school, I was afraid to fall asleep. We saw the concentration camp movie for the first time the same year as we saw the menstruation movie, in fifth grade, when I was ten. We saw them both once a year after that.

The menstruation movie was shown in the cafeteria, in a special assembly for all the fifth-grade girls. It was a secret—

the boys weren't even supposed to know what it was about. The movie was a cartoon of a talking egg. You could tell it was a girl because it had a bow on its white head. "It's too stuffy in here," said the egg. "Let me outta here!" It went down a slide and at the bottom there was a talking white rectangle called a Kotex. "I'm here to help you when you need me," it said. Every year a few boys tried to peek at our movie, jumping up to see through the window in the cafeteria door, but all they ever saw was the stupid talking egg sliding down its slide like Humpty Dumpty falling off the wall. "If you are a normal girl between the ages of eight and fifteen," said the voice at the beginning of the movie, "in a little while, a year or two, or maybe even three, something very special is going to happen to you." It was getting your period and I knew it would happen to the others, but sometimes I wondered if it would happen to me. When we were all in the girls room using each others combs and brushes to do our hair, no one offered to lend me their comb. I tried offering mine, but they all said no thank you, quickly.

"Her hair's dirty, it's got cooties," I thought I heard Mandy Sacrin whisper to Caro Warner. I worried about my hair and finally I did an experiment to find out for sure. I waited until Sidney and I were in the girl's room alone. She was brushing the knots out of her short, straight, greenish yellow hair, and I asked to borrow her brush. She shook her head no.

"You'll get it dirty," she said.

"I have to wash my hair every night," I told my mother. "It's dirty. Everyone thinks so."

"What are you talking about," she scolded. "Don't be paranoid. What do you think, they have nothing better to do all day than worry about your hair? No one is thinking about your hair." I knew my mother didn't understand because her hair was like mine, hard and dark and curly, and theirs was soft and light and straight. I must not be a normal girl, like they said in the menstruation movie, but a different kind that had wild, dirty hair like Struwwelpeter and didn't get periods. After all, I had gone to Serena and none of them had.

I bought fat pink curlers and slept on them every night,

hard and bumpy. In the morning my hair was flat and creased, but it still didn't look like theirs. "Does the Jewish race have curly hair?" I asked. "Like Negroes?"

"Don't say Jews are a race!" my mother said. "Anyone who says that is ignorant. "Being Jewish is a religion, not a race." If we were were Jewish, I didn't see how it could be a religion. Religion was something people made up to feel better, my mother had told me. They made up heaven so they could pretend they wouldn't really disappear when they died. They made up God so they could feel someone would take care of them, but really no one would. What there was instead of God was the Unconscious. Sigmund Freud had invented it. The unconscious was what made people do things, even the Nazis. *Our father who art in heaven, hallowed be thy name,* we prayed in school, and I pictured Sigmund Freud, the way he looked in that painting in the living room, hallowed and wise and disapproving. In all the pictures of God I had seen, he had a beard like that.

I wished the boys had been kept out of the concentration camp movie too, because they laughed and made pretend farts all through it. We saw that one in the gym, with just our class, and the boys' farts boomed in the big, mostly empty room. The Nazis had made the movie to record what they were doing because they were so proud of it, Mrs. Neal told us. What they were proud of was dead starved bodies piled up like stacks of limp pancakes. The ones who were alive were worse. Skeleton men with skull heads, they walked along shakily in striped pajamas, holding out their claw hands. At recess after the movie, Brian Moody, Charlie Nichols, and Chester Laughton marched stiffly around saying *Heil Hitler* and *Achtung,* and snapping their hands to their heads. Then they chased Danny Cramer and fat Jimmy Mason all around the playground screaming and calling them Jews.

When I got home I told my mother the boys wanted to be Nazis.

"They don't really," she explained. "They just acted like

that because the movie scared them. That's how boys act when they get scared."

I found out that she was right when Chester Laughton's mother shot and killed him and then herself. Mr. Lorimer came in to our class and told us about it, and Mrs. Neal put her hands over her face and cried. In recess for the next month the boys ran around the playground pretending to be Chester and Mrs. Laughton.

"Oh good, you're home from school, Chester, dear," one of them would say in a falsetto voice. "Come in and have a cookie." Then Danny Cramer or Jimmy Mason would come in, and the other one would pretend to take out a gun and start shooting. *Eh-e-e-e.* The one who was Chester would clutch his stomach and collapse. "Why'd you shoot me, Mummy?" he'd scream. "Help me, I'm dying, Mummy."

Chester Laughton had been a medium-popular boy. He could never be very popular because of the disgusting warts all over his hands, so that girls screamed if he had to dance with them in dancing school, but everyone had to agree that he was a good cartoonist. Chester had invented a thing called a basset boy that was part basset hound and part person. He'd made whole cartoon strips about the basset boys, their basset mother and father, and two basset kids. He had carved basset boys into all the desks he ever sat at. Now the basset boys looked like skull heads to me, grinning from every desk.

KILLED HER SON BECAUSE SHE LOVED HIM TOO MUCH, said the headlines of a newspaper Mandy Sacrin brought in. She said her mother told her that Chester's parents had been getting a divorce and the judge gave Chester to his father because his mother was mental. She used to be in a mental hospital, Mandy told us. Everyone thought she was better, but she went mental again and shot him so Mr. Laughton wouldn't get to have him.

You were supposed to say mentally ill, not mental. To say it like that was ignorant, like saying being Jewish was a race or saying colored instead of Negro. Still, I wondered if anyone's

mother could go crazy in the night and kill them, just like any
country could be Nazis—if it was all an accident, like my mother
said. Mrs. Laughton had been a slight, pretty woman with prematurely white hair, who always came to the PTA meetings and
plays. On Chester's birthday, a few months ago, she had brought
in a huge cake she had made in the shape of a ten-year-old basset boy. My mother had made a special cake for my birthday,
too, a ballerina with layers of purple skirts and a real doll inside that you could take out and wash and keep. I thought she
loved me just as much as Mrs. Laughton had loved Chester, or
maybe even more.

In a newspaper at about that time I saw a photograph of
a lynching. They had cut off a Negro man's penis and hung him
on a cross. In the photo he was half-burned. He looked like a
skeleton, sort of like the skeleton men in the concentration
camp movie. It was Americans who did it, Americans in white
sheets in the Ku Klux Klan. When I saw that photograph, I knew
my mother had been right, just like she always was—it wasn't
just the Germans.

After Chester's mother shot him dead, I got more and more
scared at night. I wouldn't go to sleep unless my mother was
awake and I could hear the sound of her reading or talking to
my father, or the zigzag sound of her sewing machine running.
"Don't go to sleep before me," I said to her every night,
and she had to promise that she wouldn't before I could go to
bed. When I finally fell asleep I had nightmares about Nazis and
the Ku Klux Klan, and woke the whole house up screaming.
My mother told me I was being a baby and to get control of myself, no one needed to fuss like that, even if they were asleep.
When that didn't help, she told me about the King of Denmark.
When Hitler told the Danish Jews to wear yellow stars, he said,
"Then I'm a Jew," and put on a yellow star. Then all the Danish people did the same thing, and the Danish Jews were saved.
She gave me a book called *The Last of the Just*. In every gener-
ation there was a Just Man who took all the pain of the Jews
upon himself. The last one was Ernie Levy. He was on a death

train with thirsty, dying children and he took on their pain. After I read that book I remembered how, in third grade, I had watched Sidney and Patsy mock Jennifer Thomas for being a Dainty Dot. One of them held her, and the other one tore her pink lacy dress. I hadn't done it myself, but I hadn't tried to stop them. I knew I had to be careful and never just watch something like that again. I wasn't a king, and the just men were all men, but at least I could be sure never to be a Nazi.

It was recess. I had been inside. When I came out I saw the pack of people and heard screaming. "Cooties, cooties." I came closer to see what was going on. The kids in the pack were in my class and the second-to-top class. They were all bunched around Mary Riley. They had backed her up against the red brick wall of the school and were making fat mud balls from a puddle on the path and throwing them at her.

"Cooties, cooties," they screamed, as they threw the mud. "Stinky smelly cooties." Mary Riley was crying quietly. She had snot and mud on her face. She was a tiny, black-haired Catholic girl who should have been in the lowest class with Betty Leone and Maria DeSalvo. But she wasn't, she was in the second-to-top class. Someone said she was good at Math. Everyone said Mary Riley smelled. They said you could tell the seat she'd been sitting on because of the smell. Mary Riley was a tattletale and a whiner. She never told on any popular kids, though, just on kids nobody liked, like Danny Cramer or Rocky Balducci. When Sidney wasn't around and kids screamed *Cooties* at me at recess, Mary Riley was always right in front, yelling at the top of her voice. Now, I thought, she was getting it back. All my friends were doing it. Sidney was doing it, and Sidney wouldn't do something like that for no reason. Mary had probably done something to deserve it. She had probably just told on someone. Maybe she did smell. As I stood there watching them and thinking these things, I felt my throat start to close up. I couldn't breathe. Then I knew I was feeling what it was like to be a Nazi. I jumped into the group.

"Stop it," I shouted. "You're ganging up. It's not fair." They kept on throwing the mud and yelling. I stepped in front of Mary Riley. "If you're going to do it to her you have to do it to me too," I said. After I said that, I could breathe again. My chest loosened up. I felt relieved. I wanted the kids to throw the mud on me but they didn't.

"Oh come on," Sidney said. "This is stupid." She walked off. The rest of them screamed, "Cooties, cooties, stinky smelly cooties, two cooties stick toge-ther." Then they went off in their pack.

Mary Riley stopped crying. For a moment I thought she'd take my hand, thank me for rescuing her, and ask me to be her friend. I'd have to say yes, I realized, though I dreaded the idea of being friends with Mary Riley.

"Who wants you, you stinky-old-cootie-head-Jew," Mary Riley screamed at me. "You Christ-killer-cootie-head-Jew." She picked up some of the mud on her dress and threw it at me. "Don't you come near me you stinky-old-mental-Christ-killer-Jew," she screamed. "Don't you ever talk to me again in your whole life."

It's still right, I said to myself when Sidney ignored me for the rest of the day, and all the others whispered how even smelly Mary Riley didn't want my cooties. *I didn't do it because I liked Mary Riley. I didn't do it for that.*

When I got home I told my mother what had happened. I thought she would be proud of me, like when I got an honorable mention for my poem or the grand prize at the library book report contest. I thought she would remember about the Danish king.

"What a stupid thing to do," she said. "What did you think, she'd be grateful? Of course she turned on you, they always do. If you do something like that, you're the one she'll hate the most. Who is she, anyway, that Mary Riley," my mother yelled at me, "who is she to you? What's the matter with you, you have to be a martyr? You're so strong you can stand all by yourself, so popular you don't need any friends? You have to look out for yourself," my mother screamed at me, my mother who had told me about the Danish king, my mother who knew everything. "No one else will."

WHEN THE CAMEL ANSWERED THE POLAR BEAR

"*TIC-TAC-TIC-TAC.* VERY SLOWLY, QUEEN VIC-TORIA BEGAN TO MOVE. HER CHINA ARMS JERKED. SLOWLY, slowly, she swept across the floor. *Tic-tac-tic-tac.* She headed to the foot of the stairs!" I changed my voice to make Queen Victoria the doll speak, trying to sound ancient and creaky since the man in the market had told us she was more than a hundred years old.

"Tell me who was it who laughed at me before? Who called me hollow? That person will be hollow when all his blood is gone."

"I never—," that was my little cousin, Janey, five-years old—"I never said she was hollow, did I? Did I, Catherine?"

"Let me tell them their bedtime story," I had offered, hoping to impress my newly met English relatives: my mother's dour brother, Maxim, and his elegant red-haired wife, Aunt Vivica, who had cooed over my little sister and baby brother, but seemed quite unimpressed with me. Maybe it was because she'd overheard the conversation I'd had with their son, the cousin who was nine like me, snotty, stuck-up Julian.

"I've heard you like to read," he'd told me loftily the first day we arrived. "But you won't have read a fraction of what I have. Americans don't read, do they? They do nothing but watch the telly. They don't care a jot about culture, only about money, that's what Sir said. He knows cause he's been to America, he went on Holiday. He got a first at Oxford, Sir did, and so will I when I'm a man."

"We haven't even got a telly, that's how much your stupid old Sir knows." I was generally shy with boys, but this one was related to me—and he was infuriating.

"Alright then." He cocked his head in that superior way that made me want to shake him. "I don't suppose you've read *Robinson Crusoe?*"

"I read that last year. You can ask me anything about it."

"How about *Treasure Island?*"

"Who hasn't read that!" Now it was my turn, and I tried to picture the fattest, most grown-up books I'd read. "Have you read . . . *David Copperfield?*" He hesitated, then shook his head. "How about *War and Peace?*" In fact, I had only read the love parts in *War and Peace,* skipping all the battles, but Sidney enjoyed battles, and we'd been filling each other in and acting out the best scenes, with her as Prince André and me as Natasha, so I knew I could back up my claim if pressed. Julian hadn't read that one either, so he dismissed the whole test.

"That's nothing. I know a great deal more than you. I'm three months older. And you're only a girl. Boys always know more."

"What's so special about being a boy?" I was incensed enough to hit him. "You're just saying that because I won about the books and you know I did." As we talked, I'd noticed my aunt and uncle, who'd come in from the other room, exchange glances.

"Certainly knows how to put herself forward, doesn't she,"

I thought I heard my uncle say under his breath. "Sounds so terribly American with that shrill voice, doesn't she. Doesn't really
look well in a little girl." Uncle Max had taken my mother and
me to the antique market, but then he'd gotten impatient and
complained that we were taking too long deciding whether to
buy Queen Victoria, the antique china doll, which was unfair,
because we'd had to see all the other dolls in the market before
we could be sure she was the right one. Then he'd gotten impatient again while we were in the middle of buying Victoria,
bargaining with the man who was selling her.

"Please!" he'd muttered at my mother. "Just pay what he
asks, for God's sake! The two of you sound like a couple of old
Jews. The English don't squabble over a shilling." Which was
stupid because he was my mother's brother which made him
a Jew just as much as we were, and anyway, we got the price
down by three shillings in the end, not just one. When we came
back to the house we both felt sure we had done the right thing
to pick Victoria over the others, because of her noble expression and her white wig, even though, as Julian wouldn't stop
pointing out, she was hollow from the waist down.

"It's a tea cozy!" he kept on saying." You might as well put
that old hollow thing on top of the teapot!"

"Have a go at telling them a story, darling, but I'm afraid
they'll be soon bored," Aunt Vivica had told me in her con-
descending way when I volunteered. "They'll be running downstairs in a minute, wanting their proper story out of a book."
Now Queen Victoria was getting her own back and no one was
running anywhere near the stairs. I was determined to show
Aunt Vivica that little girl or not, I could keep her children spell-
bound.

"*Tic-tac-tic-tac.*" My voice was low, hypnotic. "Victoria
was floating up the stairs." I'd read this story in a book, months
ago, but as stories did, it was changing to fit the occasion.

"I want. . ." the doll moaned. "I want—the blood of an
English boy!"

"Oh!" My eight-year-old cousin, Catherine, sounded relieved. "Watch out Nicky and Julian! You're alright then, Sylvie and Janey. It only likes to eat boys, I expect." My sister Sylvie shrugged. She was always unimpressed with my stories. My brother Nicky, who was only three, ran his fire engine along the floor, making siren noises to himself. He hadn't been listening to the story. But the cousins were proving to be a much better audience.

"Stupid old tea cozy," Julian's voice was shaky. "It couldn't go up the stairs, could it, it hasn't got any legs."

"It floated up!" Catherine contradicted her big brother for the first time since I'd been there. "Didn't you hear? Rachel said it floated up, Julian." No one moved as the story crawled to its inexorable end, with the puzzled grownups wondering in vain what could have made those strange pinpricks on the neck of their dead little boy. I felt pleased with myself and sure that Julian was looking at me with new respect. But that night I was awakened by the sound of screams.

"Mummy, Mummy, it's coming up the stairs!" I couldn't help smiling as I identified Julian's tearful, babyish voice.

"Now, now, darling," Aunt Vivica soothed him, "nothing's coming up the stairs." I fell back to sleep, but a few hours later it happened again—and again. First it was Janey, whose room I was sharing, then Catherine, in the bed next to my sister, who slept peacefully through the whole thing.

"Take it away, Mummy, take the bad doll away," they sobbed. The next morning Queen Victoria wasn't on the couch in the living room where I'd left her.

"That horrid child of yours," my uncle was saying to my mother as I entered the kitchen. "She's terrorized my children! Vivica and I didn't get a wink of sleep all night long. And you can take that revolting object and dispose of it!" He brandished poor Victoria, whose wig had come half off her head.

"I'm sure she didn't mean to!" My mother might yell at me in private, but she could always be counted on to stick up for me in front of others. Now she took Victoria from my uncle and carefully smoothed her wig back on. "Sylvie and Nicky seem to have handled it O.K. Perhaps your children are unusually sensitive.''

This was the first time that one of my stories, while admirably achieving its ends in some ways, got me in real trouble. Much more often, from the time of my earliest childhood, stories had been a source of power and delight.

I remember the bars of a crib, restrictive and high, shutting me off from the world, and a very green blanket strewn with small toys, rubber and plastic animals. I had been having a nap, or was meant to be having a nap but was now awake, and I was bored and lonely. Lying there, I put my knee up—and suddenly there was a hill. The green blanket was grass, and the white polar bear began to walk on it. I remember the polar bear well. It was a small rubber toy that could go in the bath, with one of those metal circles in its belly which must have worked as a drain, though I thought of it as a belly button. Its rubber texture was not smooth but shaggy, and after its sessions in the bathtub it no longer squeaked when squeezed, as it had at first, and its white had yellowed, just like the coat of the real polar bear I had seen at the zoo. This polar bear found itself at the bottom of the hill, on its way up, and on the other side, waiting to encounter it was the camel, the one with a hole in one of its humps where I had chewed it to find the water they were supposed to keep in there. The polar bear was surprised to meet the camel. It spoke to her, and the camel answered, and so it all started. I had learned, just like that, that stories did not only come from books. They lived inside my head, to be summoned when needed.

Stories served me well when I was by myself, but they were also useful in other situations. My mother, who, as I got older, frequently informed me that I was the most selfish, inconsiderate, dependent, and generally disappointing of children, allowed that I could always keep her amused. And while sometimes I looked at Sidney's presence in my life as simply a miracle, at other times I reasoned that that popular, desirable Sidney had first chosen me and then kept me on as her friend because, with my stories and the games I was so good at making up, I amused her too. I have always assumed that it was Sidney who picked me out, but I know now that they are often deceptive, these myths about who does the choosing. Perhaps, in fact, it was I who first selected and then carefully courted her with stories, just as I have selected and courted most of the important women in my life.

I met Sidney on my first day of school in that town. Sniffing around with the swift avidity of children and animals for a friend with whom to sustain life, I had already picked out the other new girl in the class—pretty, delicate Merrill Hollister, who wore a skimpy light blue sun dress that exposed her skinny shoulder blades, and who, terrified, threw up on the floor the moment her mother left her alone in the classroom. Merrill was even thinner and much shorter than I was, and clearly in need of protection. I approached her with some enthusiasm, but she answered my overtures by smiling shyly with her brown eyes and shaking her head no when I asked her if she wanted to play.

Rebuffed, I ventured out on my own at recess. Except for a small group playing with plastic horses on the steps, most of the girls in our class were gathered around a chubby girl in a faded green dress with a smocked front and short, straight, dark blonde hair arranged in what we called a bucket cut, implying quite literally that one's mother had suspended a bucket over one's head and cut around it. This girl was holding forth to the others, explaining that there was a mad dog loose and we were all in danger of hydrophobia, a disease her big brother had told her about. When you had it you had to have forty-four shots, right in your stomach, or you would turn into a dog yourself, snarling and foaming at the mouth, and biting everyone in sight.

"I don't see any mad dog!" That was Patsy, the ragged red-haired girl who had appeared at my house during the summer before school started, demanding to come in and play. Now she stood near the chubby girl in a propitiatory way, ignoring me as if she had never spent all those hours in my bedroom dissecting my favorite stuffed animals and pulling the arms off all but two of my dolls. "Come on, Sidney, show me the mad dog!" she ordered her friend. "Or I'm playing kickball."

"Right over there!" The girl called Sidney pointed triumphantly to an elderly collie taking itself for a morning stroll in the playground. The dog looked at us wearily and lifted its leg on a tree. Patsy snorted in disgust. "Call that a mad dog? That's just the Carr's dog, Laddy, and you know it, too, Sidney! Come on, everybody, let's play kickball. I hosie captain!"

The other girls moved off, leaving Sidney seemingly untroubled by the desertion, still gazing reflectively at the collie. Never slow to seize a chance, I ventured that we better figure out a way to get the mad dog out of the playground without touching it. The kindergarten and first grades would be coming out next, and if we didn't think of something fast, all those little kids would get hydrophobia. We had to sneak inside to get our lunches, and carefully lured the mad dog off the playground with pieces of sandwich, a dangerous operation in which Sidney took the lead—and was bitten. The doctor came in an ambulance, but before the full complement of forty-four shots could be given, Sidney came down with a light case of hydrophobia and had to run around the playground, snarling and nipping, with the doctor, syringe in hand, at her heels. In the end, right before the bell rang, President Eisenhower arrived by helicopter and awarded Sidney a medal for bravery, for saving the school and the whole town.

After that, during early recess and before school started, Sidney played kickball with Patsy, but she and I spent every noon recess—the long one—strolling arm in arm around the green park that was our playground. How long was that noon recess? A whole hour, or only half? I know that it stretched out voluptuously, the most important event in the day. As we walked, Sidney sang to me in a deep, husky voice. It was the voice of her big brother, Tom, who played the guitar and had taught her the songs, and I understood that it was Tom himself, not Sidney who strolled with me singing *it was Willy what got drowned, in the deep blue sea,* and the one about the ship Ti-

tanic, where *the rich refused to 'sociate with the poor* and were
the first to go. Then there was our favorite, *Lord Randall My
Son,* poisoned by his girlfriend but mourned by his mother who
had tried her best to warn him, but he wouldn't listen, and all
he could say to her was *make my bed soon for I fain would
lie down.*

I see now that they are all grim songs about dying, but I
didn't find them sad then or wish I could join in the singing.
Instead, as we made our slow and elderly way around and
around the playground, I experienced the kind of grace I have
felt from time to time in my life: this is where I want to be, here
in this place, with this person, and nowhere else.

Did Sidney spin her own fantasies into the fabric of the
games we made up together in the next few years? I know that
I did, and those games held some of the same excitement and
pleasure that I would later find in the pursuit of a much-desired
woman. And just as the ritual of preparing myself for the meeting—trying on clothes, rehearsing the coming scene—was almost as great as the pleasure of that scene itself, so the preparation of my room for Sidney's visit was almost as satisfying as
the visit itself.

I used the big bolsters from my bed to mark off different
areas: the slummy home of Gladiola, the sad, unpopular girl,
who lived alone and was mocked and abused; and the fancy
penthouse apartment, located high up in a chair, where Vivien,
the popular, pretty, and cruel one lived. The bottom drawer of
the bureau made a good bomb shelter, with only enough food
and water for two, which meant that someone would have to
be left out to die when the bomb fell. Sometimes, instead of
houses or bomb shelters, I prepared a blue blanket for the sea.
A tray from the kitchen was the deck of the boat, and a pillow,
covered with a yellow blanket and dotted with small, fierce
stuffed animals, was a desert island.

I would meet Sidney outside, and before she was all the way
off her bike I'd be halfway into the plot. "The bomb's about to
fall, there was an announcement on the radio about it. Vivien

and Beverly and the kids went in the shelter and locked the door. So Gladiola's all on her own, terrified. She doesn't want to ask them to let her in, but she's desperate. . . ." As I spoke I would quietly, unobtrusively slip the doll named Gladiola into Sidney's hands. "What are you doing out there?", I'd call, in Vivien's mean, stuck-up voice, as we entered the room where the scene lay in readiness. "There's no room for you in here, you bitch!" Sidney would usually be unable to resist and would end up playing dolls with me, something she was strictly opposed to in principle.

The dolls we played with had vastly different proportions. Gladiola, the chubby, little Madame Alexander doll with her round, childish limbs, looked dwarfish next to Vivien, one of the very first Barbie dolls, with her long legs, huge jutting bosom, and earrings that you stuck right through her head. The male-female couples were even more ill-matched. It was long before the time of Ken, and the only boy dolls I had were foreign ones I'd been given by friends of my mother. As partners for Vivien and Gladiola there were Kimo—a soft, floppy Eskimo of about Vivien's height but at least five times her width, pepetually dressed in brown and tan leather, with a stitched round nose and black stitched eyes, and Pierre, a French sailor doll whose hard, hollow plaster head had a chef's hat stuck onto it, and whose sausagelike body was made of painfully scratchy straw. Pierre, though more immediately appealing to the girls, always turned out to be a bad criminal type, abandoning them in the end and leaving them to be rescued by Kimo, the good and faithful boyfriend whom Vivien usually married after several episodes in which she writhed fitfully in bed or on the beach with Pierre, who insisted on having his sex in full uniform, including his hat. There were often children as a result of this union, a set of three tiny red-haired dolls whose heads had an unfortunate tendency to come off, but whom the understanding Kimo agreed to adopt, loose heads and all. It was tacitly understood that I would never tell anyone that Sidney played dolls at my house, and as I was past the proper age for this activity myself, we referred to it euphemistically as Playing Vivien. I was

aware that some children played with dolls by endlessly changing their clothes and combing their hair, but this kind of im-
becilic activity held no appeal for me. I found something in-
describably delicious about being able to be myself, outside of
the scene, and at the same time to reach into the world I'd made
and manipulate the action.

Just as Vivien could only be played in my bedroom, our
other games had definite locations and rules, but in them, instead of manipulating dolls, we ourselves acted out the parts.
The tall, white, stone horse-tying post in the driveway of the
pink mansion next to Sidney's house was the seat of the judge,
jury, and prosecutor in Electric Chair—parts played by one of
us who also had to figure out the crime. The doctor, witnesses,
and criminal—played by the other—stood in an abject posture
beneath the post and had to make up the crime. When the judge
had solved it, he chased the screaming and giggling criminal to
the electric chair, a dark cave clustered in the roots of several
tall trees, where he tickled her to death.

Sidney and I were the only two who could play Electric
Chair, but other games, like Pioneer Family and Explorers, were
much more versatile and could be played with any combination of people in any patch of woods.

My favorite game, Mental Hospital, could either be played
by the two of us or with a larger cast. It could only happen in
the basement room at my house, though, and was best played
at night. This game, like the Philosophy Club, had its origins in
one of the heavy psychology books in my mother's book
case—a grim tome called *The Mental Hospital* which described,
with plenty of juicy case histories, the workings of a state mental
institution. By the time I was ten I considered myself an expert
on psychiatry. In addition to my personal experience, which I
had no intention of sharing with Sidney, I had read Bettelheim's
Love Is Not Enough and *Truants from Life,* and I knew all about
the Orthogenic School where children whose mothers had
ruined them came to get cured. I had also carefully listened to
my mother's occasional talk about her clients, including the
reports she made into the dictaphone, in the special voice she

used for dictating, strongly accented, with lots of *ers* and *ahs*. Because it was all very secret, the clients always had letters for names. Like the sound of her sewing machine, the sound of my mother dictating was a reassuring background noise. "Er ah— Mrs. A. came for her appointment ten minutes late—," I would hear, as I drifted asleep. "Mrs. er ah A. came into the room in an er ah agitated state." Mental Hospital, in its original form, was a climax-oriented game a little like Electric Chair—the patient had to make up the problem, and the psychiatrist had to figure it out and then cure it. Unlike Electric Chair, however, sometimes doctor and patient fell in love in the end and clutched each other madly on the big double bed, the main feature of the basement room.

Mental Hospital, already an exciting game, was revitalized when Sidney and I saw a movie called *David and Lisa*—about a pair of highly attractive disturbed adolescents who lived in a kind of elegant residential hospital and who cured each other by falling in love. Somehow Sidney and I persuaded our respective parents to take us to this movie at least four times. We memorized the lines, and the two main characters became not only key players in my private fantasy life, but intrinsic to the new and improved version of Mental Hospital. Lisa, the pearl of a girl, was dark and shaggily beautiful, and because she had been abused by a wicked stepfather, spoke only in rhymes, which she used in her pursuit of David, who, because of his overcontrolling mother, was afraid to be touched, obsessed with time, and had howling nightmares about guillotinelike clocks. When Sidney and I played alone, I was Lisa and Sidney was David, but there were plenty of roles for the others during the pajama parties at my house in which mattresses covered the floor of the basement room and the only planned activity was a giant, rather orgiastic game of Mental Hospital. We were much too inhibited to experiment with sex, but we acted out our fantasy selves, switched alliances, betrayed each other, fell in love and declared ourselves—and, except for Sidney whose role as David strictly prohibited any touching, even cuddled cozily under the blankets as we never did in real life.

Just as I had secretly played with dolls long after the prescribed age, I continued to play Mental Hospital at an age when other girls were going on their first dates. It was only when I met the first of the older women whose pursuit provided me with a more absorbing game, that Mental Hospital lost its savor. Then the downstairs room became the place where I obsessively told Sidney, who was too private to share any of her own obsessions, about my progress in courtship.

REPTILES AND AMPHIBIANS

IT WAS CLEAR TO US GIRLS THAT WE WOULD
WIN THAT MORNING'S MURAL CONTEST. BECAUSE IT WAS
a contest against the boys, and consequently a matter of pride,
Sidney, who usually refused to take on such a role in school,
had stepped in and organized us, assigning each of us a reptile
according to our artistic ability. We were working hard, and our
mural showed not only the reptiles themselves, but their hab-
itats: rivers and ponds and mud banks for the turtles, jungle trees
for the snakes to coil around, and murky swamps for the croco-
diles. Out of friendship, Sidney had allowed me a crocodile, sug-
gesting kindly that most of it might be underwater. I had decided
that the body of the crocodile could be submerged, but that its
head and tail would stick out and I was pleased with my progress. Maybe it did look a little like a dog, but it was very green,
which established it as reptilian. Out of respect for the group
and obedience to Sidney, I restrained myself from using the more

exciting pink and purple paint and turning it into a dragon, a temptation I might have yielded to on my own. I didn't much care who won the contest, but I was enjoying my morning, with Sidney beside me in her spot on the long brown piece of janitor paper, looking over our mural approvingly as she waited carefully for the yellow spots on her Gila monster to dry so she could do the black.

Reptiles came in a huge variety, which we knew was why our teacher Mrs. Neal, who favored the girls, had assigned them to us, leaving the boys with the amphibians, a more primitive group which had been forced to evolve when fish got legs and tried, rather repulsively I thought, to crawl onto the land. The boys had frogs and salamanders and not much else, and they started the morning off grumbling. They'd begged for the reptiles so they could do dinosaurs, one of the only things, along with plane battles, that all boys could draw, but Mrs. Neal had said that only living reptiles were allowed and awarded them to us.

She was a very young teacher, and our top fifth-grade class was her first time teaching after graduating from college. We didn't do too much math or spelling in her class, and never any of my worst things—graphs, maps, or charts. Instead, we spent a lot of time writing stories on which we were marked for content instead of neatness and penmanship. Rather than having pop quizzes on the pilgrim fathers, whom we studied every year in history, we got to act out plays about Captain John Smith and Pocahontas. Sidney and I both loved Mrs. Neal, although only I would say it aloud, and I got the first *A*'s in my life in her class, but we didn't think of her as a *real* teacher. Mrs. Neal hadn't, like all our other teachers, started off tough for the first two weeks. Instead she'd talked about cooperating and how learning could be fun—ideas she'd picked up in faraway California, where she was from. As a result, she couldn't control the boys at all, and they ganged up and played tricks on her, laughing at her and throwing big wet spitballs whenever her back was turned, which made her shout at them and then turn red and sometimes even cry. We didn't like to see this happen, but after it had, Mrs. Neal was even more likely to say we could spend the afternoon discussing something in small groups as long as we were quiet enough that Mrs. O'Malley, the seventh-grade teacher next door, wouldn't hear us and come in. Mrs. Neal had been against competition altogether at the beginning of the year, but this was November, and she had learned what would keep us quiet.

The first interruption of our peaceful morning came when Danny Cramer scuttled over to our side, ostensibly to get a book he'd left in his desk, but obviously sent to have a look at our mural. Male enough to work on the amphibian mural, he wasn't a sufficient challenge for Sidney to set upon, so he or fat Jimmy Mason were the obvious spies. We let him go with a warning to keep away, and he went back to the boys' side to make his report. It must have been a glowing one because the next thing that happened was that Brian Moody came hurtling over to our side, and before anyone could stop him, emptied a big can of black paint all over our mural. The huge black stain covered Beryl Wong's meticulous turtle, in the very act of expelling an egg into the hole it had dug in the mud. It poured quickly over Susan Doralski's boa, which had not yet digested a goat, an obvious copy of the snake in *Le Petit Prince*, the book we'd just read in French, but good all the same; ran onto Sal Winter's splendid alligator, swimming with its baby on its head; and covered my crocodile. As it reached Sidney's Gila monster and slopped onto her shoes, we recovered from our collective gasp, and Sidney, tears of righteous anger in her eyes, sprang.

Just as Danny Cramer had been carefully chosen as spy, Brian Moody had been selected as despoiler. He was a short, wiry boy with a mean streak that made most of the other boys afraid of him, and he fought not only when he had to, as all successful boys did, but when there was no need of it, for pure enjoyment. If Sidney had not been fired by injustice, he might have had a chance, and even as it was, it was not a short fight. To the tune of Mrs. Neal's frantic, ineffectual expostulations and threats to get the principal, the shrill screams of us girls, and the equally shrill yells of the boys, the two of them rolled around on the mural, one larger but vaguely amphibious creature, streaked all over with sticky black paint. It ended, as I had never doubted it would, with Brian squealing, "Stop, I give," between sobs, as Sidney sat astride him in her torn black-spotted blue dress, threatening to give his head one last bang on the floor. She got up, examining her scratched face and scraped knee, the fruits of the righteous battle, and I was forced to share her with the others as we surrounded her with congratulations. Patsy Prud-homme, the other toughest girl in the class—but one no boy or girl would fight because she bit right through anything she could get her teeth into and would not hesitate to pick up a pair of scissors if one was at hand, actions completely outside the realm of Sidney's strict code of honor—had grabbed the boy's reptile mural and brought it over to our side. Before ripping it up, she showed it to us: a sorry thing of runny paint and baby-ish cartoon frogs with balloons coming from their mouths say-ing *ribit,* all except for Davy Cohen's outstanding red newt and Chester Laughton's excellent African leopard frog.

The noon bell rang then, signaling lunch and recess, and we heaved a collective sigh of satisfaction. Justice had been done and the morning brought to a not unsuccessful conclusion. Mrs. Neal needed to assign punishments, and then we could eat our lunch. Punishment was obligatory in the case of a fight, and we understood and accepted that teachers never bothered to find out whose fault it was but always punished both fighters equally. But Mrs. Neal, *our* Mrs. Neal, told Brian to go wash his face and eat his lunch—she thought he had been punished enough for one day. Then she turned to Sidney and told her that after lunch she was to stay in for recess. Betrayed, Sidney could only look at her open-mouthed, the tears which she had manfully held back while Brian fought her appearing in her eyes at this rank injustice.

"But you're not being FAIR, Mrs. Neal." Claiming my role as Sidney's best friend I spoke quickly before anyone else could. "He started it, you can ask anyone, he wrecked our mural for no reason, didn't you see? He just came over and poured black paint over it. Sidney was just—"

"That's enough, Rachel." Mrs. Neal was unusually firm. "I saw Sidney start the fight and I don't want to hear anything more about it."

Glad of the chance to get her to myself and to show my loyalty, I stayed in with Sidney at recess. She had been made to stay in before for lesser offenses, and it was accepted that where she went I would follow. We sat at two of the small desks, far from Mrs. Neal at her big desk by the window, but near the green plastic crate that stood at the door, its many small compartments filled with our discarded cartons of lunch milk, waiting for the janitor to take it away. Milk had come in small bottles that had to be shaken up until this year. The milk in the new little cartons was often sour, and most of us returned our milk to the milk monitor barely touched. As soon as we were settled, Mrs. Neal drew near and sat down at one of the small chairs. Attached to the desks as they were, there was no room for her long legs, and she moved to a seat on top of the desk where she loomed above us, a large female presence. She was a pretty teacher, with long, fine, light brown hair which she wore in a loose ponytail down her back, a large soft front, and a plump, sweet face, ornamented only by a light pink lipstick. This was in striking contrast to the heavy mask worn by her enemy, Mrs. O'Malley, who periodically came into our classroom, ignored Mrs. Neal, and said to us, "If your own teacher doesn't know how to make you children behave, you'll at least have the courtesy not to bother my class, who come to school to work."

Sidney and I thought Mrs. Neal was beautiful. When she bent close to us and explained that she knew we were angry at her, but she had kept Sidney in because she cared about her, not because she was unfair, our hearts melted in immediate forgiveness.

"I wanted to talk with Sidney about this," she said, "but you can hear too, Rachel. You're both getting to be big girls." She looked down at Sidney's chest, which, under the paint-stained light blue dress and the undershirt she always wore, had begun to swell, something she and I had tacitly agreed not to say anything about. "You're too old to be fighting boys now," she explained. "You're growing up, you see, and the way you were, down on the ground like that, right on top of Brian, with your dress up—well that could excite a boy, it could stimulate him. I'm sure your mother wouldn't like to see you doing that, Sidney. Now I know you didn't mean to excite Brian, but not everyone would understand...."

I looked at the floor, at the wall, anywhere but at Sidney. I knew that she, too, would be avoiding my eyes. The smell of sour milk filled me up, making me sick.

"You can go out, girls," Mrs. Neal told us gently. "I know you understand now. I know you wouldn't ever fight a boy again, Sidney."

On the playground, Sidney shrugged off Patsy, Sal, and the others girls who had flocked to her side to complain about the miscarriage of justice.

"Leave me alone," she told them, "get lost." Knowing she'd turn on me too if I stayed around her, I found our class's ongoing girls jumprope game, took an end and spun, glad of the rhythm of the rope and the mindless chant: *Susie and Jimmy sitting in a tree, K-I-S-S-I-N-G. First comes love, then comes marriage, then comes Susie with the baby carriage.*

Sidney didn't play. She never played jumprope. She stood darkly by herself all through recess and rode her bike home alone right after school instead of waiting for me the way she usually did.

We never referred to what Mrs. Neal had said again, but the torn blue dress, which had been getting short and tight anyway was replaced by a longer, yellowish one, another hand-me-down from Sidney's cousin, Chris. Sidney didn't fight a boy for the rest of the year, no matter what the provocation. She would stalk away instead. We went on loving Mrs. Neal, and when she was fired at the end of the year after we all got our report cards, Sidney and I were among the most vociferous about the unfairness of it all.

That next year, the worst year for me since I had moved to the town, I was taken out of our group and put into the second-to-top group, and Sidney and her whole family went to live in France, where her father was on sabbatical. When she came back in seventh grade no one recognized her at first. She had changed from a short, round girl with square, bucket-cut blonde hair framing her chubby pink face, to a tall, slim, pale-faced girl with long legs, bony knees, and long, lank hair of a dirty blond, slightly greenish color. She brought back with her the ability to speak such fluent, perfectly accented French that the French teacher was afraid of her, blushing and making silly jokes whenever she had to call on her in class. She also brought back a new ability to put people down, in an acid, bitter tone that no one—not the boys and not even the teachers—chose to tangle with.

THE TWELVE-LINE MAP

LOTS OF THE KIDS IN MY CLASS HAD FATHERS
WHO WERE PROFESSORS AT ONE OF THE LOCAL UNIVER-
sities. The other fathers were doctors or lawyers or in publish-
ing, and Merrill Hollister's father, who was widely admired, was
the head of a record company and once got Merrill and me free
tickets for a Bob Dylan concert. Except for my mother and
Danny Cramer's mother, who was foreign too, and was a librar-
ian, all the mothers stayed home. At the other end of the spec-
trum, in the dumbest classes, were the kids whose fathers drove
the garbage truck, worked in the dump and the town grocery
store, and plowed the town roads in the winter. Some of their
mothers cleaned the top kids' houses, and some of them packed
groceries at the local market, but most of them, too, stayed
home. Now, I guess that the fathers of the kids in the second-
to-top group must have been engineers, like my father, or sales-
men or high school teachers. At that time I didn't know, and

didn't want to know, anything about those kids. The worst disgrace for us top kids, and a threat always lurking in the background for those who struggled along at the bottom of the class, was demotion to the second-to-top class. Anything lower than that was unthinkable. If any of the kids whose fathers were professionals had trouble learning, they must have been found out early and sent away to private school—they certainly weren't around.

The one exception to the rule was weird, square-headed Merit Stone, who went to the country club dances and lived in one of the biggest and oldest houses in the town, but whose father had stood up in town meeting and said the principal had the nerve to call him and his wife in and suggest that his kid would be better off in private school and what he wanted to know was why the heck he should send his boy to private school when he paid good tax money for the most expensive public school system in the whole damn state? This speech must have profoundly shocked the mores of the town, because it was repeated at our dinner table and at those of all my friends. Mr. Stone had not only implied that he begrudged spending money for his child's education, but he had just about announced in town meeting that his son had something wrong with him. This was no news to us of course. Merit Stone threw snowballs with rocks in them that really injured people, set fires all over town, and tortured animals. He could not read, and was rumored to write not only backwards but upside-down. He was consigned to the lowest group, none of whose members would have anything to do with him, until the first week of fifth grade when he set a fire in the gym, and his parents had to give in and send him to private school after all.

While I was no Merit Stone, I was quite sure that I was the only one in our top group who didn't know what was going on in school half the time. Sidney was often bored, but she was never confused. Neither was my other friend, shy Merrill Hollister, who never talked in class and wouldn't answer if the teacher called on her, but who always seemed to get 100 on tests.

The idea that I might really belong in the second-to-top group was terrible enough, but it sometimes occurred to me that if the grownups ever found out the true extent of my confusion, they might conclude that my real place was in the lowest class of all. I tried to be a nice, sweet girl who teachers would hesitate to humiliate, and faked it when I didn't know what was going on. It was easy to avoid telling time, until my mother gave me a watch and insisted that I wear it to school. Then people kept asking me what time it was, and sometimes it was awkward to hold the watch up so they could see it instead of answering. I was glad to lose that watch and never wore another. Luckily, there were only two choices with left or right, so when I got it wrong the first time, I could pretend it was a slip of the tongue. East, West, North, and South were harder, but they didn't come up as much. Math was almost as bad as telling time and directions. I never understood anything I was doing but I had a fairly good memory, and with my mother's collusion and tutoring, I managed until sixth grade.

I still don't know what it was that caught me out. Was it that test they gave us at the end of the fifth grade, the one with the questions about if a one-legged man could carry three wheelbarrows of fertilizer for five miles in twenty-nine and a half minutes, how long would it take three two-legged men wearing roller skates? It also had science questions about un-fathomable things like planets revolving around each other, and why you lost time if you went to California and why it was warmer near the equator. That test had charts and graphs too, the complicated kind that had to be read from the side, the top, and the middle at the same time—a feat as impossible to con-template as playing the piano with one's teeth, as far as I was concerned—and those maps you had to look at and somehow mysteriously answer questions about how many people lived there, or how tall the mountains were, or how much corn they grew. I had blissfully avoided this kind of thing all year in fifth grade, earning A's for my extra-credit book reports, and adjec-tives like *Outstanding!, Original!,* and *Creative!* for my poems and stories from my teacher, Mrs. Neal. Lulled by the unfamiliar good grades, neither I nor my ever-watchful mother had seen it coming.

Possibly it was not that test, but the IQ test we were each given in the middle of the year, administered by a young lady with a warm smile who took us out of class one by one. It was to help her with her research, Mrs. Neal said, and we were to do our best to cooperate. I was glad when my turn came to take the test since it involved missing both math and gym, and I was partial to pretty young ladies and eager to impress this one. The beginning of the test was easy, and I could tell that I was coming out smart. I knew every one of the vocabulary words, and understood all about the problem with the ant and the grasshopper and why a rolling stone couldn't gather any moss. It was also easy to arrange the picture cards in the right order, with the man coming home from work carrying his briefcase first, his wife running to bring him his slippers next, and the scene with him and the three kids sitting at the table while she served them out of a big casserole dish and the dog wagged its tail in the corner, last. Then the lady gave me a smile and brought out a puzzle. The picture on the box was of a horse, and I recognized Black Beauty from the book my mother had read to me when I was six and we had both cried. I had read it to myself two more times and cried twice more. I thought I might be able to distract the lady by telling her the story of Ginger, Black Beauty's mate, and possibly make her cry, too, as well as impressing her with my grasp of psychology by recounting the way poor Ginger's years of ill-treatment had scarred her emotionally, traumatizing her for life. But the lady was not interested in the story of Black Beauty. This part of the test wasn't about remembering stories, she told me sweetly, it was about doing puzzles.

"I don't like puzzles that much," I explained, understating the case a little, but she smiled again and told me just to go ahead and do my best. She had to wait a long, long time—perhaps two or three hours, I thought—while I tried to cooperate by fitting random black pieces of horse together. I pictured my mother, and the way she would glare at me and at those black puzzle pieces lying there dead in their box. I could see her hands, grabbing up the pieces and flicking them quickly and neatly into hoofs, mane, head—an entire Black Beauty. If she had known in time, she would have taught me the skills of puzzle-making. We would have practiced on zebra puzzles, on rhino and tiger puzzles, on puzzles of Flicka and Misty and all the horses in the world, and in the end, if I had not become a master puzzle-putter-together, at least I would have been able to construct a respectable leg or mane. But they had caught us unprepared. The pieces never became even one hoof. The lady gave me an odd speculative look and told me to go on to the next thing, a pile of square wooden blocks with different colors on each side. She told me to arrange them in a pattern like the one pictured on the box cover, a task I quickly realized, somewhat comparable to the miller's daughter's assignment to spin gold out of straw. Unlike the miller's daughter, however, no little man came to help me out. I had to abandon the pile of blocks as I had abandoned the puzzle.

They called my mother into school to tell her that I was to be in the second-to-top class next year.

"You're having geography instead of history next year," she told me when she came home. It's some kind of experiment. They don't think you'll be able to keep up even though I told them I would help you every night. They wouldn't listen to me, they kept on telling me there was no difference between the two top groups, that you would both be doing the same thing. They must think I'm stupid or something!" I knew about geography—it was those maps, and how much corn was grown. It was when the teacher told us to go home and make a map of our bedrooms, and I got the yardstick and measured for a while and wrote down the numbers and then forgot what they were for and didn't know what to do with them anyway, so I drew a picture of my room, colored nicely and featuring a picture of me smiling ingratiatingly, reading a book on my chair. I always knew I had missed the point, but at least it was done and when my mother came in and found me reading, I could say I had finished my homework.

The news of my impending demotion to the second highest group didn't upset me the way it did her. I was busy worrying about the new camp she was talking about sending me to in the summer and had no room for another bad worry.

When it happened, consequently, it was something of a shock. In the playground before the morning bell on the first day of the school year, I went to join the jumprope game and the girls, the same girls I had been jump-roping with since I was seven years old, told me I couldn't play.

"This is 6D's jumprope game," Mandy Sacrin told me, "not anyone else's."

"It's nothing personal. I wish we could let you play." Biscuit Thorne tossed her long golden hair and pushed it back with her tortoiseshell barrette. "But we can't, can we? See, if we let you play we'd have to let all the other girls from 6C. Or from 6B or A or anything." They giggled at the thought of playing jump rope with Betty Leone and Marie DeSalvo, the cheap girls in 6A who were trying on make-up in their part of the playground. Behind Mandy and Biscuit I could see my rival for Sidney's affection, Sal Winter, looking down at her feet. Beryl Wong, who was turning, giggled nervously and spun her end of the rope too fast, glad it wasn't her. I moved off quickly, aching for Sidney. If she'd been there they wouldn't have dared to try something like that. But I was glad too, that Sidney was gone, safely away in France with her parents for the year, instead of here, witnessing my shame.

The new geography and English teacher, Mr. Kingfisher, was a giant. Before he'd come to our town, he'd been at Harvard, where he'd invented a new system for teaching children geography called the Twelve-Line Map. I knew right away that it was a special system for torturing me, but everyone said that those of us in the two top classes were lucky to have the chance to get him for our teacher. *A man! So tall! And from Harvard!*

"It's easy!" Mr. Kingfisher shouted enthusiastically on the

first day, bobbing around the room and waving his long arms like a clown on stilts. He paused by my desk. "None of those long faces, now." First you took your ruler and made lines up and down your paper. They had to be straight, even lines the same distance from each other, or it wouldn't work. It would have been easier to use graph paper, but we weren't allowed to; making the lines was part of the process. Then you numbered all the lines, across and up and down, and then you placed the points. Seven by twenty-five. Thirteen by four. A hundred and twenty-six by fourteen. Twenty-four points. "You'll know them by heart in no time," boomed Mr. Kingfisher. "Don't even try to memorize them, you won't need to." Once you had put in all the dots, you drew lines connecting them, and those lines magically turned into a map of the world.

Mr. Kingfisher's voice went on and on, giving instructions. I tried to understand what he was saying, but he was going too fast and seemed to be talking in a foreign language I hadn't had time to learn. My head started to throb and my hands grew wet with panic as I stopped listening to him and tried to copy the lines and dots the others were making on their papers.

"Nope," he told me, ripping my paper off the desk and crumpling it, then throwing it like a basketball player into the wastebasket at the other side of the room. "You weren't listening. Try again." By the end of the period, all the other kids in the second-to-top class had drawn a twelve-line map, and I still couldn't line my paper right.

We're doing something different this year, I wrote in a letter to Sidney. *It's the twelve-line torture.* I drew a picture of Mr. Kingfisher as a pin-headed ostrich, waving his arms around. *All the girls love him—who knows why. We had to do a composition about when we grow up and they put they wanted to marry a man six-feet-six-inches tall.* I had to watch what I wrote because if I mentioned any names, Sidney would realize that I wasn't in our real class any more. I hardly knew the kids in my new class's names anyway, and at recess I sat by myself and read a book.

The top class, my real class, had a different, special woman teacher for English, but we in the second best class had to have Mr. Kingfisher for English, too. In the second week of school he told us to write a self-portrait. I didn't want to marry him or anything, but he was a man, and I knew very few, except for my father who had told me that men probably wouldn't like me much when I grew up because I wasn't pretty like my mother. Boys never picked me in dancing school, and they would grow up to be men. All this had started to worry me. Men were important: if they didn't like you, you'd never get married or have children or have a life at all.

Mr. Kingfisher had already told us that he would read the best compositions aloud every Friday and post the best twelve-line maps on the bulletin board. He said healthy competition and making realistic judgments about each other's work was part of the process. I decided to show him that there was more to life than a twelve-line map, and more to me than the girl who always got stuck lining the paper. I would do something exceptional, something different. I would write a poem for my self-portrait. I worked hard on that poem. It had a complicated rhyme scheme as I remember, and used small letters, like e.e. cummings, for added sophistication. It was wry, self-deprecating, and revealing. I knew as I read it over to myself that Mr. Kingfisher would read it aloud, then look at me in amazement, realizing how unperceptive he'd been.

I never imagined an eleven-year-old could write a poem like this, he'd say. *I really underestimated you, Rachel. Will you accept my apology? And perhaps we ought to move you back to your real class, at least for English. That's certainly where you belong.*

"Yes," my mother agreed, as I practiced reading it to her. "He'll be impressed, alright. It's wonderful." And she gave me the first approving smiles I had seen from her ever since I'd been assigned to the low group and then ruined her summer by being homesick at camp. To make up for the smudged messes of badly lined paper and random dots and lines I'd handed in so far, I decided to print the poem with special ink on construction paper, and to illustrate it with four small painted self-portraits, one at each corner. I handed it in complacently, confident that it was a thing of beauty. But Mr. Kingfisher didn't think so. The next day he handed it back to me with a *D. Redo* he'd written in slashing red ink all over the paintings, all over the carefully lettered poem. *You must learn to follow directions.*

Back in in fourth grade I thought I had mastered the art of Never Crying In School No Matter What, once and for all. After that, I'd always managed to make it to the girls room, the crying place, well before the tears came. I hadn't even cried when they told me I couldn't be in their stupid jumprope game. Now I was crying, at the advanced age of eleven, in sixth grade, in front of a whole class of strangers and a looming giant of a man teacher.

"Never mind!" he said quickly, as appalled as I was. "You can make up your grade on the next composition. You don't have to do this one again. I guess you just didn't understand the directions." The indignity of that made me speak through my shameful tears.

"You never said," I told him, on the way out to the girls room. "You never said it couldn't be a poem."

For the first month of that year I had nightmares about the twelve-line map and woke up with a stomachache every morning. After a while, though, I settled into my state of confusion and stopped listening to Mr. Kingfisher. While the rest of the class had long ago memorized the points and gone on to take speed tests to see who could complete their map first, I filled my paper with random dots and lines and floated away to rescue Polly Carr, the eighth-grade girl I loved, from danger. Mr. Kingfisher, probably afraid I might cry again, circled warily around my desk and never called on me. Realizing that I was free, I ventured into larger-scaled scenarios, previously reserved for nighttime, in which I comforted interesting combinations of women in distress who had been trapped in bomb shelters, on desert islands, in stuck elevators, or in prison cells—dire predicaments that left them desperate for my attention and comforting touch.

My mother's frustration must have grown as I brought home nothing but papers filled with squiggly uneven lines and connected dots: maps of nowhere with a red *F* on each one. Even she must have realized that the twelve-line map, with all its intricate steps, was more than I could handle, though, because she never attempted to teach me how to do one. Instead, she saved her energy for the final project meant to demonstrate our mastery of the map-making process. We were each to make a large-scale map of the world using a different projection and showing something like population, languages, elevation, crops, or vegetation.

In a ceremonious gathering, Mr. Kingfisher met together with the two top classes and called each one of us up to the front of the room to give us our final assignment. Davy Cohen, whose scores on the speed tests were always the highest of all, and who Mr. Kingfisher seemed to love as much as the art teacher, Mrs. Antler, hated him, was called up first and got the most complicated map—the kind that looked like a balloon split eight different times down the middle. I got mine last, and it was a Mercator Projection, the easiest kind, the map for a stupid, crazy person, and all my old class was there to see my disgrace. I even hated the square, simple sound of the word *Mercator,* and would not touch the huge piece of cardboard my mother had bought me to make my map on until the night before the maps were due.

At the bitter end, my mother and I crouched together on the blond wood dining room floor, two desperate adversaries. It was late, and I wanted to go to bed and forget about the stupid map, but she was bigger than I was, and stronger willed. She had traced the outline of the world for me.

"I've done all the rest for you. Now you're filling this map in," she screamed at me, "if it's the last thing you do. All you have to do is copy it from this one in the book. You'll stay up until you finish it."

"Fine, I'll stay up all night, then," I screamed back. "And it'll be your fault if I get sick and die." Was I using colored pencils, the kind that run when they get wet, or soft, melty Cray-pas? I know that my hands were wet with sweat and unhappiness, and maybe that was what made the map smear so. Was it population I was doing? I only remember the colors: greens and browns and reds and oranges, the colors of vomit, the colors of misery, running together in a kind of blurry mess.

"Look what you've done, you've completely spoiled it. You did it on purpose, I saw you do it!" my mother screamed at me. She'd never before hit me, only shouted, but now she picked up the ruler I'd been making a weak attempt to use and threw it at my head. It bounced off and hit the map, ripping a corner. "Now look what you've done. It's ripped, you've ripped it. It's disgusting, it's a disgrace, it's a mess, you're a mess, what am I supposed to do with you? I can draw your map for you, I can work with you until I'm hoarse, but you won't listen, you won't even try. When they see this thing, they'll put you in an even lower class next year, you'll see. You'll hit the bottom of the heap and you're just doing it to upset me. You're doing it on purpose." As her voice rose to a fire engine shriek, we heard my father yawning in the doorway. He stood there in his underpants and watched her throw the box of Cray-pas which hit me, fell apart, and scattered in tiny chips all over the floor.

"Ach Gott, what's going on here, what are you two doing like crazy people in the middle of the night?" he asked us. "You want to make so that no one in this house should get some sleep tonight?"

"Make her stop throwing things at me," I whined at him. "Make her let me go to bed." I looked up at him and wished that he would stop it, would somehow comfort us both, tell us it wasn't the end of the world if I didn't get the map in on time, that he would help me tomorrow, that it was time to go to sleep. Wasn't he supposed to be my father, after all? My mother, too, looked up at him from her place on the floor. As much as I hated her then, I could feel her wanting the same thing, wanting him to say that's enough now, even to grab the map and throw it out, if only it would break the impasse.

My father shrugged, his face wearing the half smile it always wore when my mother and I fought.

"So, make yourselves sick what can I do?" he said. Then he turned and left the room, tall and hairy, his balls swinging in his white underpants. As the light came in through the window, I filled in the remaining proportions of the world.

The maps from both classes were hung in alphabetic order in a long row outside Mr. Kingfisher's room. Each one had a page underneath it with a space for everyone in both classes to enter the grade we thought that particular map deserved, and to put a comment. Afterwards they were rehung in order of merit, with the grades and comments, beginning with Davy Cohen's *A +* for his eight balloons, and ending with my Mercator with its *D*—and its surprising absence of comments. The often brutal kids must have decided that enough was enough; my map spoke for itself. The only cruel comment was the one that I myself had written, in my allotted space: *This map looks like someone got sick on it,* it said. *It's the ugliest thing I ever saw.*

I got a *D* in geography and a *C* in English, but at the end of the year my mother had a special meeting with the principal. Maybe she told them about psychology, that I'd done so badly for the first time that year because of being separated from my friends. Maybe she promised to work with me every night for the rest of her life, until we both had grey hair. Who knows what she told them. I only know that when Sidney returned the next year, a tall, thin stranger, wearing a bra instead of one of her brother's undershirts under her neatly ironed blouse, I was there, next to her in my old seat in the top class, ready to listen to her story of a boarding school in France and bookstalls by the Seine. And when, years later, it was time to go away to college, I went too, leaving behind the kids in the lowest classes who had already dropped out, or were training to be secretaries or beauticians, and the ones in the second-to-best group who stayed at home and commuted to the state university or community college.

"Tell me about last year," Sidney complained, "What did

I miss?'' I was known for my good stories, but for once I had none for her. "We did the twelve-line map," was all I could come up with. "It was boring."

IN THIS LIFE

"IN THIS LIFE," MY MOTHER USED TO TELL ME, AS IF THERE WERE ANOTHER ONE SOMEWHERE WHERE where things were different, "in this life you have to take care of yourself, nobody else will. In this life you have to fight back, otherwise they'll push you around. In this life you have to make choices."

Choices were important—I knew that. If you got tricked and made the wrong one it could ruin you forever, like in the bible story when Isaac blessed the wrong son, Jacob, by mistake when he held out a hairy goat skin that felt like his older brother Esau's hairy hands. Isaac wanted to take back what he had done, but he couldn't. He'd given his blessing and that was that, no backsies, period, final, like you said to someone who'd asked for the last drink of your soda and then wanted to give you back the empty bottle. Other people who had made bad choices were the Jews who figured that Hitler would never get them and decided to stay where they were and wait for it to be over. I pictured them in the camps before they got gassed in the ovens, standing by the fence and weeping bitterly, wishing so hard that it hurt, to make time go backwards so they could make that decision all over again, the right way this time. They reminded me of the Little Mermaid in the Hans Christian Andersen story who went down to the shoreline every night and wept because she missed the sea so much, but it was too late: Once you exchanged your fish tail for legs and left the sea to walk on earth, you could never do it the other way again.

The Little Mermaid gave away her home under the sea just to marry a human prince she'd only seen about twice and didn't even know. She should have let go of that prince, who ended up not marrying her anyway, and kept the good things she already had: her mother and grandmother and sisters and their underwater kingdom where she had her own miniature garden with red sea flowers growing like rubies in a circle. The first few times my mother read me that story, I tried to warn the Little Mermaid.

"Don't go on land, you stupid," I'd beg her, "you'll be sorry." I knew all the time it was no good, though. Hans Christian Andersen had finished the story, put it in a book, and died a long time ago. It was too late for her, and too late for the Jews, and all I could do was to be careful not to be tricked and be sure always to make the right choices myself.

At school, about the most important choice was who to have for your best friend. Since I had never wanted anyone but Sidney, that was easy. The problem was was that I wasn't alone in my choice—most of the girls in our class, even the ones who already had best friends, would have given them up in a minute for her. My most serious rivals were Patsy Prudhomme, who'd been Sidney's best friend before I came along in the second grade and who had never gotten over losing her, and Sal Winter, who was Sidney's other friend and the one she turned to when she was fed up with me. Neither of them had other best friends, so they spent all their time waiting around, ready to pounce the second I looked away. The reason Patsy and Sal still had hope was that Sidney refused to declare herself.

Being best friends was sort of like being engaged. It was only official once both of you told the others about it, but once you had done that, everyone else was supposed to keep their hands off. It was possible to steal someone's best friend from right under their nose, but it usually only happened on the first few days of school or when a new girl, who didn't have to play by the rules, arrived in the middle of the year. But Sidney would never say she was my best friend, not to me and not to anyone else, even though we were usually together at school, and everyone knew that she spent the night at my house lots of times, and that I went home with her almost every other Wednesday, which was a half day at school and one of the prime visiting times.

"Whose house are you going to?" we'd ask each other casually on Wednesday morning.

"Oh, Sidney's," I'd answer casually. "I usually do." That was pretty satisfying, but it wasn't the same as if Sidney had been willing to do the right thing and say that she was my best friend, and it didn't eliminate the competition.

Besides spending the night at her house, which, until the end of the fourth grade, I was unable to do, my only tactics for holding on to Sidney as even my unacknowledged best friend were to keep her amused, which was relatively easy, and to try not to make her mad at me, which was much harder. Asking her to say she was my best friend was guaranteed to make her mad, and so was asking her who she liked better, me or Sal. Asking her anything about her family was also forbidden because it was private. This meant that no matter how much I wanted to know, I couldn't ask Sidney what her mother had said the time she brought home the note that Miss Blanchard, our third-grade teacher, gave her when she started the Tom Boys' Club and tore Jennifer Thomas' dress. I knew that the note asked Mrs. de Toqueville to come in for an urgent conference, because Sidney and I took it out of the envelope and read it together, but I never found out anything else. For all I knew, Sidney's mother didn't even see that note. Another thing I wanted to know was whether Sidney's father ever talked to her the way I had once heard him talk to her brother Tom, when we were playing Pioneer Family and they didn't know I was hiding under the porch with the babies until the tornado passed, looking up at them through the slats.

Mr. de Toqueville had been holding up a piece of paper by its corner, as if it was dirty, and he'd said, "So that's a sample of your best work, is it? I trust you're not going to tell me you're proud of that?" and Tom, who was as tall as his father and almost grown-up, had started to blurt something out and then run inside like he was about to cry. When I asked Sidney about it, she said I was a nosy baby who was afraid to stay the night at anyone's house and why didn't I mind my own business.

I wanted to know the answers to these questions so badly that I almost lost Sidney over them. I thought if I could find out whether or not Mr. de Toqueville ever talked to Sidney like that, I'd know whether fathers were just that way—they didn't much like their children—or if it was something special about me that made my father look at me as if he wanted me to disappear. And I knew for sure that if Sidney would tell me just once that I was her best friend, I would never need to ask again. I spent a lot of time warning myself not to ask these questions, but sometimes it seemed like the harder I tried, the more sure it was that the same old words would pop out. Then Sidney would roll her eyes.

"Oh Ra-chel," she'd say in disgust, spitting my name out like something rotten she'd put in her mouth by accident, "why can't you ever leave me alone? I'm going over to Sal's after school next Wednesday. At least she doesn't constantly pester me."

Then I wished I could take back my question, but it was too late: it was out, stored up in a big, fat bundle with all the others I'd asked. I worried that the bundle would get so heavy that finally Sidney would be fed up with me, once and for all, and would choose Sal—who didn't pester her and who wasn't afraid to stay the night at her house.

Sometimes I wondered what it would be like to be the kind of best friends Merrill Hollister and Sukey Bradley were. Merrill had once said to me that they told each other everything, even things they didn't tell their own parents, and they spent all of recess with their arms around each other, whispering secrets into each others' ears. They couldn't look like twins because Merrill was short and the only girl in our class who was skinnier than me, and Sukey was the second tallest girl in the class, after Lisa Carlson, and also one of the fattest. But they tried their hardest. Some days they wore the same outfit to school: navy blue skirts and light blue blouses with butterflies on the collar, matching socks with dainty dot white frills on top, and loafers. Sidney made throwing-up noises whenever Merrill and Sukey came to school dressed alike, so I did too, even though I was secretly envious. Sidney hated buying clothes and complained when her mother made her go shopping. As soon as she got home, she tore off her dress, crumpled it into a little ball, and put on her jeans. The thought of her agreeing to wear the same clothes to school as me was as impossible as the thought of me getting an *A* in arithmetic, or getting picked first for kickball in gym, or suddenly starting to fly like I sometimes did in my dreams.

I was six-years old and stood on the threshold of the kitchen of the new house, which smelled of fresh wood and pine cones. "Do you want to help me unpack these boxes, Schnuckie?," my mother asked. At the same time my father called from the cellar where he was building a set of bookshelves. "Rachel, come to help me a minute with this?" I tried frantically to make the right choice, unable to move in either direction. I liked helping my father saw and hammer, and I hated unpacking boxes. But how could I not choose my mother?

"So go down and help him already, Rachel," she snapped at me. "It won't break my heart." I knew that neither of them cared, really, but still I felt just like the baby in the bible story about King Solomon's wisdom. In the picture, one mother held one of the baby's arms and the other mother held the other arm, and the baby had its mouth in a big red *O*, just like our new baby who was crying to be picked up. In the picture, the baby was screaming because it didn't want to be pulled apart, or maybe, I had always thought, because it wanted to keep both its mothers, not give one of them up. After a time which seemed to last forever, in which no Solomon appeared to make the decision for me, I, too, broke into sobs and pulled myself away, going into the kitchen to help my mother who was busy changing the baby and didn't want me any more. "Must you make a Greek tragedy over every little thing, Rachel?" she asked me. "You make such a big schnacks you spoil everything, for yourself too." I hung my head in shame, knowing she was right. I had no words to explain the way that in that moment of decision, life had appeared to me as a series of terrible choices, and I had been filled with sorrow at the knowledge that just as you could only have one best friend, take her or leave her, you could only have one parent.

Most dearly beloved, my mother read to me from the *Just So Stories.* And from a book of photographs called *The Family of Man. Bone of my bone, flesh of my flesh.* The blue chair where we sat and read aloud every evening had just enough room for the two of us squeezed tightly together. In the real world I had never seen my mother cry because grownups didn't, but on the blue chair we wept together for Stuart Little, who, because he was born a mouse instead of a boy, was doomed to loneliness all his life; and for the fisherman's wife who wanted too much and ended up with nothing at all because she was so demanding and didn't know when to stop asking. We wept for the elephant's child who got spanked and kicked by the grownups because of his insatiable curiosity, for the lonely boy in the red balloon who was chased by bullies, for the Little Prince who tamed a fox and a flower, loved sunsets, and was too gentle to live, and we wept especially hard for the mermaid who left the safe world of women and gave up her tail. At the end it said she turned into a daughter of air, but that was just another way of saying she died. Another one who died was the mouse in the poem who knew what kind of flower bed he needed to live in, but the doctors thought they knew better and kept persuading him and persuading him, until after a while he didn't know what he wanted anymore and he gave in and said O.K. to the wrong kind of flowers, and then when he got them he died from unhappiness. My mother and I always cried when we came to the last lines: *The dormouse lay happy, his eyes were so tight / He could see no chrysanthemums, yellow or white, / And all that he felt at the back of his head / Were delphiniums (blue) and geraniums (red).* It was like the way the boy in *The Red Balloon* became happy all of a sudden after the bullies' stones had knocked him to the ground, right before he went up in the sky with the red balloon. And the way the Little Prince at the end got happy right before he jumped off his planet to his death. We would start crying as soon as they started with that kind of happiness that always meant someone was about to die.

Lots of the books weren't sad at all, but even when they were, I didn't mind. I loved sitting close to my mother, smelling her hair and feeling the warmth of her, and unlike the foolish Little Mermaid, I knew when I was well off. I was determined to hold on to her, and nothing—not my father, and certainly no stupid prince—was going to make me let go.

"*Scheuszlich*," my father snarled, pacing past us and giving me a disgusted, mean look the way he always did when we read together, "Ach Gott, is *scheuszlich,* how you two make yourselves hysterical for nothing." My mother and I turned our wet eyes away from him and drew closer together, safe on our sad island where he wasn't allowed to come. He must have known she wouldn't answer him because she never did when she was reading to me, but after walking back and forth a few times and banging things in the kitchen, he always tried to talk to her. I thought maybe it was like me with Sidney: he knew he shouldn't, but the words jumped out of his mouth. Sometimes I felt sorry for my father because of the way she refused to answer him when we were reading, and because he was only a man who my mother had had to marry in order to have me and my brother and sister. He was not the bone of her bone and the flesh of her flesh like I was, and any time she got tired of him she could stop loving him and leave him, and then, as all three of us knew, he would turn into foam, float away on the balloon, curl up in a little ball like the dormouse, and die.

Although I felt sorry for my father, in this life you had to look out for yourself. Just as being Sidney's best friend meant an unceasing battle against Sal Winter, whom I would have liked under other circumstances, being my mother's most dearly beloved meant being my father's enemy. There was only room for one of us, and when I got up from the blue chair he would grumble at me under his breath so she couldn't hear, "Ach, why can't you leave your mother alone for once. Why are you always there?" The look he gave me when my mother and I read together, or when she made me go over my multiplication tables with her all evening, or when I ran to tell her my day as soon as she got home from work, quickly, before he could get to her, made me wonder why he didn't sneak into my room at night and smother me with a pillow or a nylon stocking like the Boston Strangler. He was so much bigger than me, he could have done it if he wanted to. I couldn't really picture my father doing that, but I could imagine him taking me sailing and, accidentally on purpose, leaving me behind on some tiny island in the middle of the ocean. When he got home he would tell my mother, *I tried to stop her but she wanted to go off on her own. She insisted, what could I do? So take care of* me *now. Read to* me!

One reason I wasn't really scared was I knew that if he ever did try to get rid of me, my mother would would turn her face against him and stop speaking to him, the way she did to me when she wanted me to spend the night at Sidney's. In the end, he would have to go back to wherever he had left me and grab me up—cold, frozen, and almost dead from hunger—and return me to her.

If my father had tried to maroon me on an island when he took me sailing, or in the dark woods with only bread crumbs to find my way home, I would have fought him alright, but I would have understood. After all, I never asked him to join us on the blue chair. But my father didn't drop me off anywhere, even though he had plenty of chances. Instead, when we went skiing, he lifted me up so the chair lift wouldn't hit my back, and when we got to the top of the mountain, which would have been a perfect place to leave me, he skied down slowly in front of me in long, wide zigzags so that when I followed in his tracks I couldn't possibly fall. In the summer, he swam next to me all the way out to the float, and when I said I was tired he let me hold onto his shoulders—which were furry like Esau's hands in the story—and towed me back. Because I was the only one in the family besides him who never got seasick, he sometimes took me far out on the sailboat, and instead of deserting me on an island, the way I thought I might have done with him if I had had the chance, he told me stories of hiding from the Nazis. When we went sailing we ate special delicious sandwiches he made for us, filled with wurst and lettuce and tomatoes and pickles and cheese, all sliced very thin, and he taught me songs in French: the one about the two companions who fought over a girl but only one of them could have her and so they turned into enemies and killed each other. And, *Chevaliers de la table ronde, goutons voir si le vin est bon. Goutons voir OUI OUI OUI, goutons voir NON NON NON. Goutons voir si le vin est bon!* When I was with my father at the top of a mountain or in the middle of the lake or out in the middle of the sea in the sailboat, sometimes I forgot you could only have one parent and I would ask him questions. "Do you think I'm pretty? Did you like my poem?"

He would smile and that mean look would come into his eyes. "You'll never be pretty like your mother," he would tell me, and "You'll never be as smart as her, so don't even try." Then I had to remember that even though my father would not kill me or leave me in the deep dark woods to die, he had chosen, just like I had, and that if I ever let him he would cut me and my mother apart.

In the daytime it was alright. They went to work and I went to school. I loved to go to other peoples' houses in the daytime, and I liked to stay for dinner and eat other people's strange food.

It was in the nighttime when bad things could happen—when the Nazis came for the Jews, when the Boston Strangler struck, and when my mother and father went in their room and shut the door. That was the time I knew I couldn't be away from her. "Don't go to sleep before me," I always told my mother right before I went to bed, and when she answered, "I won't," I knew we had a deal and no one could cut us apart during the night.

There was one part of the Little Mermaid story that was so horrible I always forgot about it until my mother started to read it, and then I would scream for her to stop and put my fingers in my ears: the part when the witch cut the Little Mermaid's tongue out. It was bad enough to have someone cut your tongue out under protest, but the way she opened her own mouth on purpose for the witch to do it was what terrified me. After that, of course, she couldn't talk. When the prince stopped loving her she couldn't do anything but sit there and look at him sadly. I knew that if I gave in and let anyone persuade me to spend the night away from my mother, I would be just like the Little Mermaid—opening up my mouth for them to cut out my tongue.

It was my mother herself who finally persuaded me to spend the night at the de Toquevilles, after all of Sidney's taunts had failed to move me. "What a baby!" Sidney said, when she got mad at me for asking her something I shouldn't have. "And you're the one who's always talking about best friends. How can you have a best friend when you won't even stay the night?"

"Tell me how come you won't?" It was Patsy Prudhomme on the morning school bus. "How come you're scared to spend the night? I spent the night at Sidney's house when I was five years old and you're nine. You must be mental, just like everyone says."

"Just do it." My mother looked hard into my eyes, trying to hypnotize me. "What's the matter with you? Don't you want Sidney to be your friend? Don't you want to have any friends?" I could put up with this, but after awhile she stopped reading to me. "You're too old now," she said. "You're too clingy. You know how to read, anyway, you can read on your own." Then, at bedtime, when I asked her not to go to sleep before me, she turned away and wouldn't answer. "You're too old for these rituals," she told me. "Leave me alone." After a week or two of this, I asked Sidney if I could spend the night at her house that Friday after school. "Don't do it if you don't want to," she'd said when I'd asked her if I could stay the night. "I mean, don't force yourself. If you're going to make some kind of big deal of it, just forget it."

Usually I enjoyed having dinner, which they called supper, at the de Toquevilles. I liked the white tablecloth and the candles and the slightly scary moment when Mr. de Toqueville looked around the table, deciding whom he would pick to say grace. He hadn't asked me yet, but I was ready just in case he did, with the same prayer Sidney always said, *Godisgreatgodis-goodandwethankhimforourfoodA-men.* I liked the ceremony of grace and the moment of silence afterwards when I would open my eyes a slit and watch all the de Toquevilles, even Tom, sitting there with closed eyes talking to God. I also liked the way Mr. de Toqueville's voice boomed out during dinner, and the funny stories he told about stupid people at work and the mistakes the president had made. Usually I even liked the strange food they had—one dried-up pork chop or lamb chop without sauce, lumpy mashed potatoes or watery rice, and frozen peas that had shriveled up in the water. Dessert was the best— gingerbread or chocolate cake that Mrs. de Toqueville baked herself instead of the store-bought desserts we had at home. Tonight I couldn't get any of it past the lump in my throat, though. It was a big hard lump that had started growing at school during the day and had gotten bigger during the afternoon, when Sidney and I played Electric Chair on the white stone horse-tying post outside. When it was my turn to be the criminal, my mind had gone blank, and I hadn't been able to think of a good crime.

"Biscuit Thorne's body was found in the girl's locker room strangled by a gym suit," I'd said finally, but my voice had sounded squeaky and weird like someone else's voice, and Sidney had stared at me and sighed in a fed-up way.

She figured out the crime too easily, and when she shouted "Electric Chair!" and it was time for me to run, my feet felt like they had weights on them and I let her catch me right away and throw me into the hollow between the two big trees.

"Let's not play any more, you're no fun today," Sidney had said, and I'd wanted to answer, "I've changed my mind, I'm going home," but I knew that I couldn't. It was too late for that.

Mrs. de Toqueville had called us in then. "Now Margaret Sidney, you and your little friend go straight upstairs and wash your hands for dinner." It was the same thing she always said, in the same slightly sarcastic voice, and usually I liked it. But this time it had sounded cruel, and I'd wondered if she was really making fun of me.

"Now, deary, what's the matter, don't you like the supper?" Mrs. de Toqueville asked me. All the de Toquevilles stared at me and I swallowed the piece of dried-out lamb chop, feeling it make a hard lump in my neck that was stiff from trying not to cry. I wondered if they could see it going down from the outside, like when a snake swallowed a cow.

"I'm not very hungry," I croaked. "I have a stomachache." Because of my stomachache, I didn't eat the gingerbread Mrs. de Toqueville had made especially in my honor for staying overnight the first time. She sent us up to bed early, and we lay side by side in the two hard beds in the guest room.

"Let's at least play something," Sidney suggested, but I couldn't answer her. "It's only one night," I told myself, but time had stopped, and I knew it would never be over. I would never be able to go home again, either, because there was no more home. "Don't worry, you won't have to spend the night again because I'll never invite you," Sidney hissed.

Was it much later when I finally started to cry? I think it was, because Sidney had to wake up her mother. Did she take me into the bedroom where Mr. de Toqueville lay in bed with blue pajama bottoms on, or was it Mrs. de Toqueville who led me in there? I remember the shame of seeing Sidney's elegant father lying on the big bed snoring with his mouth open. Mrs. de Toqueville had a sleeveless nightgown on, and I could see her skinny chest and her bare wrinkled arms that looked like my grandmother's. She had a curler in the front of her hair. These were the most private kinds of things, I knew, things Sidney would never forgive me for having seen.

"Now, now, don't fuss like that, you're a big girl," scolded Mrs. de Toqueville. She reached out to pat me, and I shrunk back. "I hate to bother your poor mother at this hour. Why don't you try to go back to sleep? You'll see, it'll be morning before you know it." But the possibility of relief had emboldened me.

"I could walk home," I whispered. Sighing, Mrs. de Toqueville told me to get my things together while she dressed. Back in the guest room, Sidney lay facing the wall, pretending to be asleep."

"Say good-bye to Rachel, dear, I'm just going to run her home," her mother told her, but Sidney did not turn over.

My mother wouldn't speak to me that night. The next morning she told me she had never been so ashamed in all her life as when Mrs. de Toqueville turned up with me in the middle of the night.

"That settles it," she said, "this summer you're going to camp." I knew I had spoiled everything and that I would have to pay for it, but for the moment I didn't care. The summer was too far away to be real, anyway. The important thing was that I had saved myself in time. No one had cut out my tongue. I was home.

BEAU
SOLEIL

THE CAMP WAS CALLED BEAU SOLEIL, WHICH
MEANT BEAUTIFUL SUN, BUT THE GREY CEMENT BUILD-
ing with ornamental porches that only the staff was allowed on
was not beautiful by any standards, and I soon realized that the
name was a kind of sarcastic joke, a trick like those bad dreams
I'd always had in which adults held out a present, smiling, while
all the time they meant to kill you. Or like what had happened
to my father when he lived in France and won the ski competition and the men in charge said *congratulations, now you can
come with us and enroll in the ski patrol.* And when he believed them, and went with them, they grabbed him and put
him in a concentration camp.

"So how come they dropped you off here, you skinny little rat?" The big American girl fingered my shorts and snorted.
"What'd they pay for these, five dollars? What're your cheap-

skate parents doing, anyway, getting divorced?"

"No," I said, pulling away from her sharp fingers. "They just wanted me to go to camp and learn French." I knew this camp was my punishment, but I wasn't about to say that to this mean girl, who must have been at least thirteen, or to the others forming a circle around me. With their smooth linen playsuits, simpler and more stylish than any clothes I'd ever seen, and their hard, grown-up faces, they were like no kids I'd run into before.

"Learn French, huh! I bet they told you they'd be back for you in a month or two," a younger one said, looking at her friend for approval.

"They *will* be back. I'm just staying six weeks, then they're coming to pick me up." They all laughed knowingly.

"That's what our parents said to us, didn't they. And we're still here."

"Come on, girls, leave it alone. It's so naive it makes me want to puke," the first girl declared. "Not worth our time." She turned to me in a final spurt of venom. "Look, stupid, if they really wanted to send you to camp, they would have picked a real camp, an American one, right? In case you can't tell, this isn't a real camp, it's a school for rich girls that stays open all summer so none of our so-called parents have to bother with us. I hope they left you plenty of cash for the help, anyway."

"They already paid," I whispered. "They sent in the money." She shook her head, taking a bill out of her pocket and shaking it in the air. It looked bright and pretty, like made-up money. "*Les pourboires,*" she said. "Tips. Or into the *dortoir* you go, with all the little Frenchies. We Americans have rooms of our own. We don't have anything to do with them, and we don't want anything to do with you, either, so keep out of our sight from now on. I don't want to see you hanging around us any more, get it? Or we'll really give you something to cry about."

Ever since the time I had been brought back from the de Toquevilles in disgrace in the middle of the night, my mother had been talking to me about this special Swiss camp she'd seen an advertisement for in the *New York Times*. As the end of school approached and summer got nearer and more real, we did nothing but argue about it. Her plan was for the whole family to fly to France together, where they would put me on a bus for the camp. Then the rest of them would take a train to a village on the Spanish coast, where they and the English cousins had rented a big house for six weeks. Until it actually happened, I thought my mother would change her mind. I couldn't believe she actually intended to send me away and make me miss all that.

"Don't you want to be the best one in your class in French?" she kept on saying. "Girls come to Beau Soleil from all over the world to learn French for the summer." She showed me the brochure they had sent, a picture of smiling girls sitting around a grownup, under a tree. "You'll love it there, wait and see, it's a famous camp, it's very expensive. You want to go, really, you just don't know it yet. You don't want to come to Spain and sit on the beach with six-year-olds. All the others are younger than you, you'd be bored to death, you'd be begging me to send you to camp in an hour."

"Julian's going to Spain. He's three months older than me. They're not making *him* go to camp," I protested.

"So now Julian is your best friend, you love him so much all of a sudden? All the two of you did last time was argue and fight over who was smarter and better read. And now you're dying to spend the summer with him? Well, I don't want you two arguing in my ears the whole time. Anyway, you want to go to camp, you said so before. You want it all, you always want it all."

"But I don't, Mummy, I don't want it all!" I felt myself getting confused—swept away under her flow of words just like the dormouse in the poem who knew that he needed to sleep in a nest of delphiniums blue and geraniums red but the doctors kept convincing him that he wanted chrysanthemums until finally he agreed and it killed him. I tried to hold on to what I knew. "I never said I wanted to go to camp, why would I say that? You're the one who wants me to go, not me."

"You did, you begged me to go, don't deny it now!" My mother was so outraged she was beginning to convince me that she must be right. She paused, and when she spoke again it was in another voice, almost pleading.

"Don't you see, Schnuckie, you can't cling to me forever, afraid to spend a night without me, not even able to go to bed without bringing me into your neurotic rituals. I can just picture you, thirty years old, still afraid to leave home, with no life of your own, no family, still making me crazy, still torturing me. Ach, it's a nightmare, it's enough now. I don't need you nagging at me in Spain too, I need a rest. You'll see, in the end you'll be glad I sent you."

"Couldn't you persuade her not to make me go? Couldn't you at least try?" I begged my father. He shrugged his shoulders. "So, did the world maybe come to an end that you suddenly come to me? You know she's in charge." My sister and brother grinned at each other, glad to get rid of their bossy big sister and have our mother to themselves for once. I knew that the whole family had hardened itself against me and was determined to push me out. There was nothing I could do.

I was in the big, high-ceilinged *dortoir*, with its row of beds. My own bed was exposed, set out right in the middle of the floor. I lay under the too-small, too-puffy quilt, crying into my long roll of pillow shamelessly. The French girls were throwing my hairbrush from bed to bed, screaming whenever it hit their own.

"Oh, *que c'est sale! Que ça pue!*" I couldn't speak much yet but I understood enough to know they were saying that it was dirty, that it smelled, and so did I. They got sick of that soon, and started on the next thing. "*Elle a pissé dans le lit, l'Amerloque! Venez voir, venez voir, Mademoiselle, elle a pissé dans le lit!*" The mean French lady, Mademoiselle, must have known by now that I had not and would not pee in the bed, but she came in on cue, just like she had all the other nights, sniffing the air and wrinkling up her nose.

"*Quelle bêtise*," she scolded me in French. *Behaving so, crying like an infant when your parents spent good money to send you to camp!* She turned to the girls. *What babies these Americans are with all their money! Those others like little queens, turning up their noses as if they're too good for us. And now this one, meowing like a wet cat! Spoiled, all of them, that's their trouble!*

It seemed to me that this same scene had already happened more times than I could count, and that it would go on happening, over and over, every night until the end of time. I was being punished for being afraid to spend the night away from home, for shaming my mother in front of Mrs. de Toqueville, for all those years of being a bad, crazy girl who had to be sent to Serena, for being too clingy, too dependent, and too needy, for torturing my mother and driving her crazy. It was not that I really believed that my parents had abandoned me here forever, as the other American girls' parents had apparently done. It was more that the six weeks that stretched in front of me could have been six months or six years as far as I was concerned. I could not see the end of it. My pride gone, I cried all the time—on the long promenades in a double line through what I remember as constant wet rain; at night in that exposed bed; standing by the window watching the rain; sitting in my place at the long table, not eating; or standing in the courtyard, watching the games, which always seemed to involve knocking someone down on the cement. It was as if my other life had gone, as if Sidney and the others at school and Polly Carr and my favorite books and the library and our house and my dog Dusty who followed after me on my bike, had all vanished and I was left alone, in the dark tunnel of my nightmare.

The smell of bananas had made me want to throw up my whole life, and a taste of oranges and apples was enough to make me gag. At Beau Soleil they had decided that the spoiled Ameriloque who would not eat the good fruit set in front of her would sit there until it was all gone. I sat at the wooden table waiting for time to pass. I didn't mind if I had to sit there all day. It was better than standing in the courtyard or going on those long, tiring promenades, walking in line next to a partner who held her nose and complained loudly. I didn't care if they set the same fruit in front of me at the next mealtime. I wasn't hungry anyway.

"*Mais qu'est-ce que c'est alors! Elle ne mange pas du tout!*" the ladies whispered in the French I was beginning to hate even as I understood more and more of it. *She never eats, she'll get sick, the parents will blame us.* After they had scolded me for ungratefulness and let me sit at the table from one meal to the next a few more times, they gave up and delivered me to the American counselor. He was a stout, not very young man, with colorless blond hair which grew sparsely on his head and more heavily, like damp, curly fur, on his legs and forearms. He wore khaki shorts and a khaki shirt, and his short, pink, hairy legs and arms popped out of his sleeves and pants like the swollen pale sausages that were barbecued on the outside grill once a week for a special *pique-nique.* I remember his whole head being a purplish red, too, maybe because the sun sometimes shone at Beau Soleil after all, and it had burned him, or maybe because that was the way I usually saw it.

His name was Bill, and he had been hired for the American girls, who would have nothing to do with him, and who slammed and locked the door of their bedroom when he tried to go in there, pushing the big bureau up against it. No one else would talk to him either, and I had seen him wandering disconsolately around the concrete playground. Bill's misery, which disgusted me because it reminded me somehow of my own, and something raw and vulnerable about him had made me avoid him so far. Now, however, the French ladies brought me to him and closed the door behind them.

Bill beckoned me over to where he sat in a large plastic chair. I came to him, and he pressed my awkward, gangly eleven-year-old body onto his lap, grasped each of my arms with his strong hands, and told me over and over again to stop crying, it would be alright, I was such a sweet girl, why didn't I relax and let him comfort me? He comforted me by rubbing and bouncing me against the hard swollen bump inside his khaki shorts. My tears dried, I stared straight ahead and watched his head get more and more purple until he gave a sort of groan. "There there, don't cry," he mumbled again, as his hands loosened and I backed away. I was wet, and there was a smell, just like the girls had been saying. "Come to me whenever you feel homesick," Bill told me. "I know how you feel. They're not nice people here, but I'm your friend."

"You see!" the ladies scolded me. "Bill had to treat you like a little baby, a big girl like you, to cry all the time! Aren't you ashamed?" I was ashamed, and I hated Bill more than the ladies and wished he would die, even though, as he had told me himself, he was my only friend there. I was disgusted by the person I had turned into in that place, thin and tired, constantly crying, and hating the only person who was nice to me.

"Please," I begged my mother on the phone to Spain. "You have to let me come there. I can't stand it here. I'll be good, I won't be clingy, I won't even talk to you. I have to leave, I'm too homesick, I hate it here." It never occurred to me to mention Bill.

"From all the way there you're doing it," my mother screamed at me. I hated her for thinking everything I did was about her, but couldn't hate her because I missed her so much. "Don't call me any more if you're just going to torture me," she went on. "You're staying for the six weeks we decided on, and that's that, so you might as well get used to it." I could tell she wouldn't give in, so I asked to speak to my father. "Daddy, it's not just me, it's a horrible place, really, I promise, I'm not exaggerating. They say I pee in the bed, they make fun of me, they hate me here." I could tell he understood, but his voice laughed at me from Spain over the phone. "She's the one you always go to. She's your mother, me I'm no one. It's too late to come to me now."

As the weeks went by I seemed to turn to stone inside. I started to eat a little, and I made a sort of friend, a little bewildered Greek girl of eight or nine, with honey-colored skin and hair, who had no one at all in that place who spoke her language, and who clung to me wordlessly and held my hand tightly on the long promenades. I had mostly stopped crying, but Bill still found me every day and offered comfort on his bulging lap.

When my parents came to get me in a rented car, I had said good-bye to Ariadne, and was waiting on the doorstep with my things. Although I had longed to see my mother, when she arrived neither of us held out our arms. We looked at each other once and then away. She went to find the American counselor —the one who, the director had told her, had been so nice to her daughter, had taken hours to comfort her when she was homesick and wouldn't stop crying. I refused to come with her and went to sit in the car, turning away from my father's shame-faced hug and his offer of Swiss chocolate.

"You knew," I accused him. "You knew what it was like and you wouldn't help me." I was ready to be angry at my mother too, but I couldn't—she was too angry at me.

"Quite an achievement," she said, as he drove away, before I could say anything. "You ruined my summer, all the way from Switzerland you managed it. I hope you're satisfied."

For a while I accepted my mother's version of the summer I ruined for her. Later, I invented a new version of those months, in which I did not stay at the camp for more than a few days. Instead, sometimes with the Greek girl, sometimes alone, I ran away like kids in books did, hitchhiking through the country, sleeping in barns and making friends, getting on a train bound for Spain, doing whatever I needed to do to leave that place behind me once and for all. Every time I remembered the summer the way it had really been, I felt ashamed. I vowed that if I ever felt like that again, anywhere, for any reason, I would not stay around until someone came to get me. No matter if it was the middle of the desert and the middle of the night, I would leave right away, on my own. No one could keep me there.

LOEV

MY GRANDMOTHER, OMA, SAID IT ALL THE TIME,
COOING IN HER GERMAN ACCENT. "OPA LOE—VS YOU SO-
o-o much," we imitated her, making the word sound long and
oily the way she did. When she said that about him, Opa just
sat by with his face hard and stony. He was my father's father,
a tall, straight man with icy blue eyes who rarely spoke and
never seemed to listen to what Oma said. "Who is the best Opie
in the whole world?" Oma asked my sister and brother and me.
"Who is the Opie who loe—vs you so-o-o much?"

My other grandmother, who was just called Grandmother,
and who was a speech therapist, was also fond of the word.
"Which grandmother do you love more, me or Oma?" she asked
us, grabbing us fiercely by our chins to make us speak in the right
way. "Both the same," my sister and I always answered, but my
little brother, who didn't know any better, shouted out "Oma!"

"It's your own fault, Mutter," my mother would scold her.

149

"You see what happens when you ask such questions to the children?"

A Baby Is Born, the sex book my mother had read me when I was five, and again when I was seven and ten, used the word, too. *When a man and a woman love each other very much,* it said, *they lie down together and the man's penis goes into the woman's vagina.* I pictured them lying there side by side, stiff as boards, waiting for it to happen, and knew for sure that it had nothing to do with me.

In the books my mother read to me, love was often dangerous. It could get you into bad trouble, like it did the Little Mermaid, who felt sharp needles were being driven into her feet. I knew about those needles from the way it felt when my mother was disappointed in me, or from when Sidney looked at me with contempt, but my kind of love wasn't about sharp needles, any more than it was about penises and vaginas, the fake sweetness of Oma's voice, or the harsh eagerness of Grandmother's. Still less was it about the ritual of dancing school.

"Ladies Choice," boomed the man dancing teacher. "It's all yers, girls." There was a scratch when the vulture lady in the black dress put the needle back on the record and we girls got up and scrambled as fast as we could toward the object of our choice. Ladies Choice was a refinement on the ordinary torture of dancing school, and it demanded instant action. I headed straight across the floor toward carrot-haired Charlie Nails, a tall, skinny, painfully shy boy who emerged from obscurity every year to win first prize in the science fair for his complicated electric machines. Charlie Nails' hands were always dripping wet, and he never spoke at all or even looked at me as we promenaded around the room, faking dance steps and trying to avoid the glance of the dancing teachers, but he had never refused me yet, following me onto the dance floor meekly every time I picked him in Ladies Choice. I dodged in between the horse girls, already dancing smoothly with their partners, to the seat where Charlie slouched like a flaccid rubber band. Right before I got there, though, Merrill Hollister, who'd been sitting on his side of the room, slid neatly into place in front of him. I watched the two of them shuffle onto the gym floor, heads down.

If you missed your chance in Ladies Choice, you were in trouble—at least if you were me. My other option had been Bill Adams, the nicest, handsomest, and most athletic boy in our top class. Bill was the only boy in our group who had friends from the lowest groups whom he knew from being captain of the soccer and softball teams, and actually invited to his house. He was so popular that he could even risk dancing with me, and he had never turned me down either, but I could see Bill dancing with Kai St. Clair, whose notebooks had *Mrs. Bill Adams* and *Mrs. Caroline St. Clair Adams* written all over them, and whose silver-studded mouth was now stretched in a wide, horsey smile. In fact, I realized, all the boys had been claimed but Danny Cramer, Jimmy Mason, and Brian Moody. "Keep away, ugly," Brian hissed at me, as if I would ever pick his hateful self in a million years. The only other girl left, Susan Doralski, picked Danny Cramer, who groaned loudly so the other boys would know it wasn't his fault. That left Jimmy Mason, who never even tried to dance right, but spent all his time trying to trip people, dragging his partner after him. Jimmy, who looked like an overinflated beach ball, was certainly in no position to refuse me. But he saw me coming and zigzagged out the door, squeezing between the dancing couples. "Godda go to the basement" he explained to the vulture lady.

All the boys, even Brian Moody, were gone now, and the lady was coming towards me, mincing along in her black high heels which reminded me of the claws on a bird of prey. Those shoes had stepped on me so many times since I started going to dancing school every Tuesday afternoon two years ago, in fifth grade, that just looking at them sent flashes of pain up through my legs. She had sharp nails, too, which she dug into my skinny shoulders as she dragged me onto the gym floor. "One two three, one two three," she shouted in my ear. "Listen to the rhythm, dear, I've told you before. Eyes on your partner's left shoulder. Don't watch your feet, they can take care of themselves." I knew from experience that they couldn't, so I pretended not to hear her and kept my eyes on the floor, trying to anticipate those sharp heels.

"How was it tonight?" My mother drove me home from dancing school, full of hopeful questions. "Did they appreciate your dress?" I had on my new dancing school dress, a store-bought one from Flanagan's. It was made of a glistening silvery material and had a full skirt and black velvet sash. My favorite part was the rosebud attached to the chest. It was deep crimson, made out of a softer silkier stuff than the dress, and I loved to stroke it. When I'd tried on the dress in Flanagan's dressing room, it had seemed clear to both of us that a girl wearing a dress like that, with a rosebud like that on it, would have to be picked.

"No one picked me again," I told my mother. "And no one would dance with me in Ladies Choice, either. I had to dance with the lady. How come I can't quit like Sidney did?"

"So go ahead and quit if you want to. I told you before, I'm not forcing you," my mother assured me. "If you want to be a quitter that's fine with me. And grow up not knowing how to dance so no one will ever ask you out on a date in high school or your whole life long."

I tried to picture myself on a date in high school, dancing with some tall boy who looked like Sidney's brother Tom. It would have to be a new boy from somewhere else who didn't mind my hair. Maybe Polly Carr would be at that dance too. I pictured her in the low-cut light blue dress she'd worn as Elizabeth Barrett Browning in the high school play, the one that showed an expanse of white chest and a startling cleavage. She'd come to the dance with Peter Livingstone, the handsome tenth-grader who had played Robert Browning in the play. But he'd gone off with another, thinner girl, a slim blonde horse girl who looked like Biscuit Thorne.

I quickly brushed off my partner and followed Polly, as she ran stumbling across the dance floor, accompanied by giggles and whispers. I found her in the girl's room, sobbing

*against the towel rack. "Never mind him," I told her as I came
in. "You're worth ten of him. You're worth a hundred of him!"
Polly Carr turned to me with her large blue eyes, so startling
against her black hair and white skin, still streaming tears.
"Why did you bother to come after me, Rachel?" she asked. "I
thought no one cared." I held out my arms and she moved into
them. Her skin was soft and warm against mine. "It's funny,"
she mused, "he doesn't seem to matter that much any more."*

"Come," my mother prodded me. "We're home. Go change
so we can eat." The smell of pot roast made my mouth water
as I took off the silver dress and my panty girdle, breathing
deeply while I rolled the tight, lumpy thing off me, and checking
my thighs for the bruises it always made. In fifth and sixth grade
we'd worn white socks, but now that I was twelve and in seventh, we had to wear panty girdles and stockings with our black
pointy party shoes. Even though I was always hungry and ate
more than anyone in the family, I still only weighed seventy-
four pounds, so my mother had had to take a tuck in the panty
girdle to make it stay up. The slippery tan stockings always hung
in wrinkles around my ankles by the end of dancing school. I
knew that by the time the marks of the panty girdle and the sore
place on my foot from where the vulture lady had stepped on
me had worn off, it would be Tuesday again. But maybe it would
be different next time.

"Do you think I could get a blue dress like the one Polly
Carr had in that play?" I asked my mother as I came to the table. "For my next dancing school dress?"

"That girl has a figure like a forty year old matron," my
mother snorted. "Not a lovely slim figure like you. You don't
need a dress like Polly Carr's!"

"Ach, here we go again," my father said. "Do we have to
hear every dinnertime about Trolley Car?"

"Trolley Car, Trolley Car!" screamed my little brother. "Rachel
loves Trolley Car!"

"Don't call her that," I told him, but not very angrily. I was
always looking for an excuse to say Polly's name out loud, and

although I wouldn't admit it, I especially liked it when my father or brother called her Trolley Car, or my mother said she was fat, and I had to defend her against their slurs. I liked the feeling that I was the only one who knew the real Polly Carr. I really *did* know her. She had even talked to me once, when I was in fifth grade and she was in seventh like I was now, and we both won a prize in the school poetry contest. Polly had won first prize, like she always did, and I won the honorable mention and got to go up on stage with her to read my poem, "Canada Geese." I can still remember that poem, which was easy to recite because of its catchy rhythm. I had modeled it on "The Charge of the Light Brigade," my mother's and my favorite poem. "Half a league, half a league, half a league onward!" we would shout together until my father said, "Ach Gott!" and put his hands over his ears. "Forward the light brigade! Theirs not to reason why, theirs but to do or die."

Canada geese, Canada geese, my poem went. *White flash over the water! White heads, red beaks, Canada geese, Canada geese.* Polly Carr's poem, which was also about nature, didn't rhyme at all, and I resolved that my own poems never would again. Her delivery was slow and thoughtful, and I knew that I would never forget the way her deep drawling voice sounded, or the way she stared seriously out at the audience, curving her lips in a half-smile as she read about the mist rising over the river at dawn. Standing next to Polly in the front row of the auditorium, waiting to read our poems while the principal, Mr. Lorimer, made a speech about our school's creative talent, I could smell the perfume of her raven black hair, and after I read my poem she smiled right at me. "Well read, Rachel!" she said. "With spirit!"

Everyone knew that I loved Polly Carr, my whole family and everyone in our class, and I would have been proud for the whole school to know. When my mind seemed to get stuck on all the things I hated to think about—dancing school, being ugly, the terrible thing I'd said to Sidney which would probably make her decide to never be my friend ever again, how to stop my mother finding out that I had failed the make-up math test—it

made me feel better to think about Polly. No one ever mentioned
that I was supposed to think about Peter Livingstone and not
Polly Carr at night, and no one told me that Ladies Choice at
dancing school was a preparation for anything but that magic
time when I would suddenly wake up and realize that I was no
longer the skinny worry girl with funny hair who was afraid
to leave home and whom no boy would dance with. When that
time came, I would look in the mirror and see a real American
girl, the kind my mother wanted, who got thrown into the lake
by boys, got asked to dances, and had straight, sleek, long hair
like Polly Carr's, or that beautiful new folksinger, Joan Baez's.
It would be a relief when that time came, and if going to dancing school could make it happen, I was willing to keep on going, especially since I didn't want to give up getting new dancing school dresses. Still, I knew that all that had nothing to do
with love. Love was about Polly Carr or about Adele Smith, the
sad lady with strawberry blonde hair who had once gone skiing with us and who I could still smell when I closed my eyes,
even though that ski trip had happened two years ago. Love had
nothing to do with boys, not even handsome, almost grown-
up ones like Peter Livingstone, or Sidney's brother Tom, who
was going away to college next year, and who used to say,
"Don't let 'em get to you, Rach! You'll show 'em all in a year
or two." I thought I might marry Tom when I grew up, if Sidney would let me, but I couldn't imagine wanting to think about
him at night or on the school bus, or during all those precious
times when I was alone and beautiful Polly Carr cried in my
arms and told me she loved me—she had just never realized it
before.

By the time I got to high school, Polly was a senior and rumored to be going out with the blond music teacher, Mr. Ashley, who lived with the art teacher, Mr. Hammer. It seems clear
to me now that if Mr. Ashley was interested in any student at
all, it was more likely to have been Peter Livingstone than Polly
Carr, but then I was convinced that the two of them shared a
profound but star-crossed love. These days when Sidney stayed

overnight and we slept together in the double bed in the basement room, we abandoned Mental Hospital in favor of a new game. Polly and Mr. Ashley took place in the dark, and began when the silence was broken by me, calling out in Polly's voice, "Oh, Mr. Ashley!"

"Oh, Polly!" Sidney would respond in Mr. Ashley's deeper, but equally fervent voice. "What shall we do?" Occasionally I persuaded Sidney to play Polly, which was more exciting in a way, except that then I had to be silly Mr. Ashley whose eyebrows were frozen in a perpetual sarcastic leer, and who conducted opera, humming and *zinging* under his breath during silent study hall. I don't believe that Sidney and I ever touched during Polly and Mr. Ashley. Nevertheless, it was a deeply stirring game which left me lying awake for hours afterwards. Only on the nights when I was alone in bed was it possible to eliminate Mr. Ashley altogether and, by switching parts with lightning speed, achieve my goal—to both be and have Polly Carr.

By the time I met Marina Finch I was a senior, and Polly had long ago departed for college. By then I had already achieved one considerable victory. All through junior year, Sidney (silently) and I (vocally) had loved Mrs. Levine, our dark intellectual young English teacher, whose biting wit was a grown-up version of Sidney's own, and whose long, black hair, confined in a tight bun, was rumored to reach her waist when she let it down. In the spring, Sidney and I got our drivers' licenses, and Mrs. Levine, who was pregnant with her first child and was not returning to school the next year, invited us to drop in on her when we happened to be in town. Sidney declined, sensing condescension, but I was soon a regular on Mrs. Levine's living room couch—an attentive, sympathetic presence, who drank in the stories of voter registration in Mississippi and activism in Chicago like the finest wine, kept my visits short, was quick to lend a hand with the dishes, and brought along the book—which I had just happened to run into—that Mrs. Levine had mentioned wanting to read on our last visit.

As the days grew warmer, we moved to the front porch.

Mrs. Levine asked me to call her Irene and began to let her hair, which indeed reached her waist, down in my presence. On one memorable afternoon, she tearfully confided to me how afraid she was that having the baby would detach her from her world of politics and ideas and turn her into nothing but a boring housewife. While that afternoon's events represented the apogee of my career, and I replayed and embellished them night after night, I knew on some level that Mrs. Levine-Irene was not quite my cup of tea. She was too capable, too straightforward, too avidly intellectual. She even reminded me a little of my mother, who had taken to her right away when she met her. I knew, in fact, that she was quite capable of rescuing herself.

Did Mrs. Levine know all this too, and was it with some sense of my predilection for dark, rounded, older women, soft and vulnerable enough to need rescuing, that she set me up with Marina Finch? It was before our summer friendship, during the last week of school, that she called me into her classroom and introduced me to the teacher who would be replacing her, another very young woman with long, dark hair fastened on her head with one of those leather barrettes with a kind of spear through it.

"This will be Miss Finch's first teaching job," Mrs. Levine told me with that deadpan, just slightly sarcastic look which made me know she was really meant for Sidney, not me. "Watch out for her next year. Make sure she's alright, O.K.?" Then she turned to Miss Finch. "Rachel knows her way around," she told her. "She'll look after you." Having set the scene quite splendidly, she left the room. My initial impression of likeness between the two women faded immediately. While Mrs. Levine's hair always stayed firmly in its tight bun unless she let it down, lots of Miss Finch's had already escaped from its confines and hung in little wisps around her round face. Miss Finch was rounder altogether than even a pregnant Mrs. Levine, and the long, flowing purple cape she had draped carelessly over one of the desks marked her, in my eyes, as a hippie. I had recently replaced the dating, diving model of womanhood for this new ideal, vaguely constructed from Joan Baez, Joni Mitchell, and Mrs. Levine's Civil Rights movement stories. The new model, which like the old one, required long, straight hair and popularity with boys, felt equally inaccessible. Still, I was pleased to note in Miss Finch certain marks of imperfection—long runs in her stockings and the way the zipper of her skirt kept easing down so that she had to pull in her stomach and zip it up again.

"Will you be teaching mostly honors classes, like Mrs. Levine?" I asked her. She shook her head vehemently.

"No way! See, I've got real problems with this tracking system you have here," she said. "It's like, I'm most interested in the kids who get stuck in the bottom tracks, the ones everyone gives up on by the time they're ten, you know? They need me more than you honors kids. I really wanted to teach in the inner city this year," she confided. "But I just graduated, and everywhere I applied they said to get some experience first. So when they hired me here, I asked if I could have all the so-called lowest classes, and they were thrilled, you know? I guess it was a kind of unusual request."

"I'm in the lowest class in Math," I volunteered, pleased that this shameful fact could work in my favor for once. "And when I graduate from college I'm going to teach in the inner city myself." This idea had never exactly occurred to me before, but now I realized it had been there all along, at the back of my mind. Irene Levine had already receded to the background. I was deeply and instantly in love, and my experience in math class—where Maria DeSalvo made out with Rocky Balducci, Eddie Leone read dirty comics, and no one but me even bothered to pretend to listen to poor, mousy Mr. Rudi—made me wonder hopefully whether Miss Finch might be in need of my rescue services next year.

When I knocked on the door of her classroom after the last bell on the first day of the new school year, there was no answer. I peered through the little window at top and saw Miss Finch sitting at one of the kids' desks. Although her back was to me, her slumped figure, her head cradled in her hands, and her hair, which had almost completely escaped the leather barrette, told the story—along with the blackboard, whose dull green surface was peppered with the biggest, juiciest collection of spitballs I had ever seen. I knocked again, then opened the door a crack and asked if I could come in. Turning slightly, so that I could see her face crumpled and wet with tears, Miss Finch nodded.

"It'll be alright," I told her. As I got a paper towel from the sink in the back and cleaned the board of the loathsome spitballs, some of which contained not only spit but bubble gum and something else that might have been snot, I felt that by now familiar tightening of the chest and gloried in the chance to do something really disgusting for her.

"Don't worry, I've been around those kids for a long time," I told her. "I know them. We'll figure out what to do."

Unlike Mrs. Levine who had waited until the semester was over to offer me Irene, Marina and I were on first-name basis from the beginning. "She's so beautiful!" I moaned happily to Sidney. "She lives alone, but she has this boyfriend, Mike, who sometimes stays with her. She doesn't know if he really loves her, though. He's a dancer, and he's bisexual. She thinks he might really like men better. And she has two cats—a black one and a white one—and they're named Freedom and Now. When she smokes grass she lets them inhale some, so they can all get high together."

"Oh, *please.*" Sidney had named her own cat Henry. Like Mrs. Levine, she thought people who took drugs were boring. "I bet she has verses from *The Prophet* up on her wall!" she went on. "And one of those plaques that says, *If you love someone, let them go.* Anyway she shouldn't be telling you all that, not about smoking grass and her bisexual boyfriend and everything."

When I picture myself in Marina's apartment I am standing at the sink, one of those old-fashioned white enamel ones with a tiny window above it, doing her piled-up dishes. I am aware with every inch of my body of Marina Finch behind me, pacing and talking. *You don't know what's going on do you, Mister Jones,* screams Bob Dylan on the record player. I sit in the other room after finishing the dishes, with Marina pacing around me, smoking a cigarette and telling me about her life. There are clothes tossed on the bed and the chairs, corduroy skirts and peasant blouses with tassels, jeans she tells me she'll be able to get into after she loses a few pounds. Marina sews, but not like my mother does, or how we learned in Home Ec. She makes up her own patterns and sews unlikely things together—sequins and feathers and bright scraps of fabric. It is a place full of a vital, slightly hysterical energy, of things left un-done, of eating binges, crises, tears, and cigarette and marijuana smoke and confidences. For me it is thick with a sexuality I do not recognize, but which makes my chest ache and my cheeks throb and tickle. It is as far as I can get from my mother's house.

"Oh, I forgot," Marina tells me. "I wanted to show you my new dress. I just finished it." She goes into the bathroom and comes back wearing something colorful—red and purple on black velvet—one of her patchwork of scraps. I think it looks great on her, but she is seized with despair.

"Goddamn it to hell, the fucking thing's too small. Look at me, fat and flat, the titless wonder! No wonder I don't turn Mike on. Don't worry, it's O.K. to have small breasts if you're thin, like you are," she explains to me in a kindly aside, "and it's even sort of O.K. to be fat if you have big breasts, see, then you're the Earth Mother type. But here I am, the worst possi-ble combination—fat stomach and tiny breasts!" She rips off the dress, tearing it, and now she is standing in her jeans, facing me. I see nothing fat or ugly, just her gently swelling, full pink belly, her perfect, small rounded breasts with their hard, tight little nipples. I sit there absolutely still, looking at her, trying to get my breath, which won't come. "You're not fat," I finally get out. "You're just right."

Is it something fervent in my tone that moves her away, makes her grab and hastily put on her cream-colored bra, dirty at the edges and held together with a safety pin, then pull her blouse over her head and change the subject? Or is it, instead, my stillness, my apparent lack of response? I know about homosexual men now, because she's told me all about her boyfriend, Mike, and about Mr. Hammer and Mr. Ashley, but I have never heard of homosexual women, and it doesn't occur to me that what I long so much to do, reach out and touch her, is a real possibility in the world.

In fact, I was not entirely ignorant of the existence of lesbianism. Mademoiselle Pirignon, a middle-aged French woman with short, scrubby hair dyed an improbable white-blonde, briefly taught our honors class during the first half of sophomore year. Mademoiselle wore tight skirts, knee socks, and men's button-down shirts, with three buttons left open, and she had a faint but noticeable mustache. Everyone knew she loved Patsy Prudhomme, who had changed overnight from a wild and ragged tomboy into a glamorous though still-ragged girl whose eyes were always half-closed and who all the boys in the school panted after. When, at Mademoiselle's suggestion, we drew names out of a hat for our Christmas present grab bag, we all noticed the embarrassing way Mademoiselle cheated, sifting through all the names in the hat until she got Patsy's. The present she bought, a creamy silk blouse, was much too good, and obviously cost more than the two dollars Mademoiselle had told us we could spend. Patsy's father made her give the blouse back, and Mademoiselle did not return after Christmas vacation. This left us with old Miss Mercer who was really a Latin teacher and never gave us anything but grammar to do for French. No one said the word lesbian out loud, and middle-aged women did not interest us enough for lengthy gossip, but there was a certain amount of giggling and whispering.

French teachers were a notorious bunch anyway, always leaving in the middle of the year. Freshman year we'd had another one, Mr. Trojanian, who told us that he was grateful to have gone to a teacher's college and we were all rich snobs who didn't appreciate our chances. He especially hated Sidney, whose year in France had left her with an accent far better than his own. Once he came into the room when she was imitating him speaking French, and after that he kept making jokes about how in French, everything had a *masculin* and a *feminine* gender, except for some people who were in somewhere in between, eh, Mademoiselle de Toqueville? After that, it was war. Sidney started correcting his pronunciation, and he'd ask her if perhaps she competed with men because she wished to be one? There was always an uncomfortable silence when he said something like that. I knew that Sidney's honor had been insulted somehow, and I wanted to defend her, but since I wasn't sure exactly what he was getting at, I didn't know how. Eventually it was easy to persuade the rest of the class that since Mr. Trojanian didn't really know how to speak French the right way, it would better to ignore what he said and to spend French period playing with the sets of colored blocks the lower sections used for New Math.

Thin and soft spoken, daintily dressed, and not competitive with boys—who did not interest me—I was never accused of being masculine, and at least consciously, I never associated the murmurings and rumblings surrounding our French teachers with my own love for women, or with my growing relationship with Marina Finch. In the spring, when I had been accepted to college and was already on my way out of that town and that school, she took me with her to Washington to go on a Civil Rights march where Martin Luther King, Jr. was to speak.

Every night for the past weeks, I have rocked myself to sleep in Marina's little red sports car. I have smelled her perfume as she leaned over me to get something. I have felt her hair glowing against my face.

Now I'm really sitting here, and it's spoiled. My period started a few hours ago, and between the wrenching cramps and my fear that Marina will wrinkle up her nose and ask what that bad smell is, I wish I'd never come on this trip. Worst of all is the growing necessity to tell her that I need to stop and change my tampax. I only started to menstruate at fifteen, a year and a half ago, and my periods are still unpredictable, disappearing for months at a time and then returning with terrible pains, which I feel vaguely ashamed of, as my mother always says that women who complain about their menstrual cramps are making a big fuss about nothing and giving men an excuse to keep women out of high positions. I have no idea whether or not Sidney gets cramps because, as she considers the subject in bad taste, it is one we do not discuss. I have accordingly never compared notes or even spoken of bleeding with anyone. I am convinced that Marina will despise me if I say the words. It will be worse if I keep silent though, so finally, blushing and stumbling, I blurt out that I've got my period and I need to stop at the next rest stop.

Marina pulls up at the rest stop and produces some magic pills that immediately stop the cramps. Back in the car, for the next hour or so, she free associates about menstruation.

"I bleed so goddamn heavily," she tells me, "I have to stick in two supers at once. But the blood still comes out the edges." Then she is talking about grief, about breaking up with a boyfriend. "I cried so hard," she says. "I was driving, and it was pouring. I could hardly see and I couldn't tell if it was the rain or the tears blocking my view."

Oh please, I can hear Sidney's voice, and my mother's, *Ach, such a fuss, so self-indulgent, she should pull herself together.* But for me the little red car is full of blood and tears, of release and ease and most wonderful femaleness. *I love you,* I want to tell Marina, but instead I talk about my looks, my hair, how boys don't like me, how I wish they would. Marina says she was slow starting with men, too. There's nothing wrong with my hair— curly hair might even come into fashion one of these days— and anyway, I'm lucky to be thin. I'm an attractive woman, really. Who knows, maybe I'll meet someone in Washington. That would be good for my self-confidence, which is half the battle anyway. She pulls out a joint, telling me it helps her to drive, and offers me a drag. I take it wet from her lips, and I want to hold the sweet taste in my mouth forever. Now the smell of grass fills the car—comforting, harsh, and forbidden.

In Washington, we march with her friends, men with

beards and women with long straight hair who say fuck a lot and treat me like one of them, and after a while we hear the voice of Martin Luther King, Jr., echoing magnificent and holy, over the microphone. I wander off by myself for a while, and, knowing that this will please Marina best, I find a skinny yellow boy, a year or so younger than me, with an enormous Afro. We run up along the side of the march until we are almost sure we have seen Martin Luther King's back, and then I invite my new friend back to Marina's friend's place, where everyone is crashing. When we get there, we both smoke some of the dope that's circulating, and then we kiss, just like the others are doing, curled on the sofa and rolled in blankets all over the room. I can feel Marina's approving glance on me, and I try to get the boy to stay longer, but he says he has to get home, his mother didn't want him to go to the march in the first place, she's going to worry, and after a while he leaves. I see that Marina, deserted by the man she was with, has fallen asleep on the sofa in her jeans and shirt.

Do I unzip her jeans for her before I go to sleep? Do I cover her up? I don't remember that, only the feeling of ease and luxury which goes with knowing that I am far from home, that the car is small, with only room enough for the two of us, that the trip back from Washington is a long one, and that there is plenty of time for my own kind of love.

Other titles from Firebrand Books include:

Artemis In Echo Park, Poetry by Eloise Klein Healy/$8.95
Beneath My Heart, Poetry by Janice Gould/$8.95
The Big Mama Stories by Shay Youngblood/$8.95
A Burst Of Light, Essays by Audre Lorde/$7.95
Cecile, Stories by Ruthann Robson/$8.95
Crime Against Nature, Poetry by Minnie Bruce Pratt/$8.95
Diamonds Are A Dyke's Best Friend by Yvonne Zipter/$9.95
Dykes To Watch Out For, Cartoons by Alison Bechdel/$6.95
Dykes To Watch Out For: The Sequel, Cartoons by Alison Bechdel
  /$8.95
Exile In The Promised Land, A Memoir by Marcia Freedman/$8.95
Eye Of A Hurricane, Stories by Ruthann Robson/$8.95
The Fires Of Bride, A Novel by Ellen Galford/$8.95
Food & Spirits, Stories by Beth Brant (*Degonwadonti*)/$8.95
Free Ride, A Novel by Marilyn Gayle/$9.95
A Gathering Of Spirit, A Collection by North American Indian
  Women edited by Beth Brant (*Degonwadonti*)/$10.95
Getting Home Alive by Aurora Levins Morales and Rosario Morales
  /$8.95
The Gilda Stories, A Novel by Jewelle Gomez/$9.95
Good Enough To Eat, A Novel by Lesléa Newman/$8.95
Humid Pitch, Narrative Poetry by Cheryl Clarke/$8.95
Jewish Women's Call For Peace edited by Rita Falbel, Irena
  Klepfisz, and Donna Nevel/$4.95
Jonestown & Other Madness, Poetry by Pat Parker/$7.95
Just Say Yes, A Novel by Judith McDaniel/$8.95
The Land Of Look Behind, Prose and Poetry by Michelle Cliff
  /$8.95
Legal Tender, A Mystery by Marion Foster/$9.95
Lesbian (Out)law, Survival Under the Rule of Law by Ruthann
  Robson/$9.95
A Letter To Harvey Milk, Short Stories by Lesléa Newman/$8.95
Letting In The Night, A Novel by Joan Lindau/$8.95
Living As A Lesbian, Poetry by Cheryl Clarke/$7.95
Making It, A Woman's Guide to Sex in the Age of AIDS by Cindy
  Patton and Janis Kelly/$4.95
Metamorphosis, Reflections On Recovery by Judith
  McDaniel/$7.95
Mohawk Trail by Beth Brant (*Degonwadonti*)/$7.95

Moll Cutpurse, A Novel by Ellen Galford/$7.95

The Monarchs Are Flying, A Novel by Marion Foster/$8.95

More Dykes To Watch Out For, Cartoons by Alison Bechdel/$7.95

Movement In Black, Poetry by Pat Parker/$8.95

My Mama's Dead Squirrel, Lesbian Essays on Southern Culture by Mab Segrest/$9.95

New, Improved! Dykes To Watch Out For, Cartoons by Alison Bechdel/$7.95

The Other Sappho, A Novel by Ellen Frye/$8.95

Out In The World, International Lesbian Organizing by Shelley Anderson/$4.95

Politics Of The Heart, A Lesbian Parenting Anthology edited by Sandra Pollack and Jeanne Vaughn/$11.95

Presenting. . . Sister NoBlues by Hattie Gossett/$8.95

Rebellion, Essays 1980-1991 by Minnie Bruce Pratt/$10.95

A Restricted Country by Joan Nestle/$8.95

Sacred Space by Geraldine Hatch Hanon/$9.95

Sanctuary, A Journey by Judith McDaniel/$7.95

Sans Souci, And Other Stories by Dionne Brand/$8.95

Scuttlebutt, A Novel by Jana Williams/$8.95

Shoulders, A Novel by Georgia Cotrell/$8.95

Simple Songs, Stories by Vickie Sears/$8.95

Speaking Dreams, Science Fiction by Severna Park/$9.95

The Sun Is Not Merciful, Short Stories by Anna Lee Walters/$7.95

Tender Warriors, A Novel by Rachel Guido deVries/$8.95

This Is About Incest by Margaret Randall/$8.95

The Threshing Floor, Short Stories by Barbara Burford/$7.95

Trash, Stories by Dorothy Allison/$8.95

The Women Who Hate Me, Poetry by Dorothy Allison/$8.95

Words To The Wise, A Writer's Guide to Feminist and Lesbian Periodicals & Publishers by Andrea Fleck Clardy/$4.95

Yours In Struggle, Three Feminist Perspectives on Anti-Semitism and Racism by Elly Bulkin, Minnie Bruce Pratt, and Barbara Smith/$8.95

You can buy Firebrand titles at your bookstore, or order them directly from the publisher (141 The Commons, Ithaca, New York 14850, 607-272-0000).

Please include $2.00 shipping for the first book and $.50 for each additional book.

A free catalog is available on request.